Agatha Christie [is known] as the Queen of [Crime. Her] detective novels and books of stories have been translated into every major language, and her sales are calculated in tens of millions.

She began writing at the end of the First World War, when she created Hercule Poirot, the little Belgian detective with the egg-shaped head and the passion for order – the most popular sleuth in fiction since Sherlock Holmes. Poirot, Miss Marple and her other detectives have appeared in films, radio programmes, television films and stage plays based on her books.

Agatha Christie also wrote six romantic novels under the pseudonym Mary Westmacott, several plays and a book of poems; as well, she assisted her archaeologist husband Sir Max Mallowan on many expeditions to the Middle East. She was awarded the DBE in 1971.

Postern of Fate was the last book she wrote before her death in 1976, but since its publication two books Agatha Christie wrote in the 1940s have appeared: *Curtain: Poirot's Last Case* and *Sleeping Murder*, the last Miss Marple book.

Agatha Christie's *Autobiography* was published by Fontana in 1978.

Books by Agatha Christie

The ABC Murders
The Adventure of the Christmas
  Pudding
After the Funeral
And Then There Were None
Appointment with Death
At Bertram's Hotel
The Big Four
The Body in the Library
By the Pricking of My Thumbs
Cards on the Table
A Caribbean Mystery
Cat Among the Pigeons
The Clocks
Crooked House
Curtain: Poirot's Last Case
Dead Man's Folly
Death Comes as the End
Death in the Clouds
Death on the Nile
Destination Unknown
Dumb Witness
Elephants Can Remember
Endless Night
Evil Under the Sun
Five Little Pigs
4.50 from Paddington
Hallowe'en Party
Hercule Poirot's Christmas
Hickory Dickory Dock
The Hollow
The Hound of Death
The Labours of Hercules
The Listerdale Mystery
Lord Edgware Dies
The Man in the Brown Suit
The Mirror Crack'd from Side to
  Side
Miss Marple's Final Cases
The Moving Finger
Mrs McGinty's Dead
The Murder at the Vicarage
Murder in Mesopotamia
Murder in the Mews
A Murder is Announced
Murder is Easy
The Murder of Roger Ackroyd
Murder on the Links

Murder on the Orient Express
The Mysterious Affair at Styles
The Mysterious Mr Quin
The Mystery of the Blue Train
Nemesis
N or M?
One, Two, Buckle My Shoe
Ordeal by Innocence
The Pale Horse
Parker Pyne Investigates
Partners in Crime
Passenger to Frankfurt
Peril at End House
A Pocket Full of Rye
Poirot Investigates
Poirot's Early Cases
Postern of Fate
Sad Cypress
The Secret Adversary
The Secret of Chimneys
The Seven Dials Mystery
The Sittaford Mystery
Sleeping Murder
Sparkling Cyanide
Taken at the Flood
They Came to Baghdad
They Do It With Mirrors
Third Girl
The Thirteen Problems
Three-Act Tragedy
Towards Zero
Why Didn't They Ask Evans?

Novels under the Nom de Plume of
'Mary Westmacott'
Absent in the Spring
The Burden
A Daughter's A Daughter
Giant's Bread
The Rose and the Yew Tree
Unfinished Portrait

Books under the name of Agatha
Christie Mallowan
Come Tell Me How You Live
Star Over Bethlehem

Autobiography
Agatha Christie: An Autobiography

Agatha Christie's Poirot

BOOK TWO

FONTANA/Collins

This collection first published by Fontana Paperbacks 1990

This collection © Agatha Christie 1990

'The Cornish Mystery' was first published in the
United States in *The Underdog and other Stories*,
1951; 'The Veiled Lady', 'The Adventure of "the
Western Star" ', 'The Lost Mine', 'The Kidnapped
Prime Minister', 'The Disappearance of Mr
Davenheim' and 'The Adventure of the Cheap Flat'
were first published in *Poirot Investigates*, 1925; and
'Double Sin' was first published in the United States
in *Double Sin and other Stories*, 1961.

Phototypeset by Input Typesetting Ltd, London
Printed and bound in Great Britain by
William Collins Sons & Co. Ltd, Glasgow

CONTENTS

THE CORNISH MYSTERY

'Mrs Pengelley,' announced our landlady, and withdrew discreetly.

Many unlikely people came to consult Poirot, but to my mind, the woman who stood nervously just inside the door, fingering her feather neck-piece, was the most unlikely of all. She was so extraordinarily commonplace – a thin, faded woman of about fifty, dressed in a braided coat and skirt, some gold jewellery at her neck, and with her grey hair surmounted by a singularly unbecoming hat. In a country town you pass a hundred Mrs Pengelleys in the street every day.

Poirot came forward and greeted her pleasantly, perceiving her obvious embarrassment.

'Madame! Take a chair, I beg of you. My colleague, Captain Hastings.'

The lady sat down, murmuring uncertainly: 'You are M. Poirot, the detective?'

'At your service, madame.'

But our guest was still tongue-tied. She sighed, twisted her fingers, and grew steadily redder and redder.

"There is something I can do for you, eh, madame?"

'Well, I thought – that is – you see – '

'Proceed, madame, I beg of you – proceed.'

Mrs Pengelley, thus encouraged, took a grip on herself.

'It's this way, M. Poirot – I don't want to have anything to do with the police. No, I wouldn't go to the police for anything! But all the same, I'm sorely troubled

7

about something. And yet I don't know if I ought – '
She stopped abruptly.

'Me, I have nothing to do with the police. My investigations are strictly private.'

Mrs Pengelley caught at the word.

'Private – that's what I want. I don't want any talk or fuss, or things in the papers. Wicked it is, the way they write things, until the family could never hold up their heads again. And it isn't as though I was even sure – it's just a dreadful idea that's come to me, and put it out of my head I can't.' She paused for breath. 'And all the time I may be wickedly wronging poor Edward. It's a terrible thought for any wife to have. But you do read of such dreadful things nowadays.'

'Permit me – it is of your husband you speak?'

'Yes.'

'And you suspect him of – what?'

'I don't like even to say it, M. Poirot. But you do read of such things happening – and the poor souls suspecting nothing.'

I was beginning to despair of the lady's ever coming to the point, but Poirot's patience was equal to the demand made upon it.

'Speak without fear, madame. Think what joy will be yours if we are able to prove your suspicions unfounded.'

'That's true – anything's better than this wearing uncertainty. Oh, M. Poirot, I'm dreadfully afraid I'm being *poisoned*.'

'What makes you think so?'

Mrs Pengelley, her reticence leaving her, plunged into a full recital more suited to the ears of her medical attendant.

'Pain and sickness after food, eh?' said Poirot thoughtfully. 'You have a doctor attending you, madame? What does he say?'

'He says it's acute gastritis, M. Poirot. But I can see

that he's puzzled and uneasy, and he's always altering the medicine, but nothing does any good.'

'You have spoken of your – fears, to him?'

'No, indeed, M. Poirot. It might get about in the town. And perhaps it *is gastritis*. All the same, it's very odd that whenever Edward is away for the week-end, I'm quite all right again. Even Freda notices that – my niece, M. Poirot. And then there's that bottle of weed-killer, never used, the gardener says, and yet it's half-empty.'

She looked appealingly at Poirot. He smiled reassuringly at her, and reached for a pencil and notebook.

'Let us be businesslike, madame. Now, then, you and your husband reside – where?'

'Polgarwith, a small market town in Cornwall.'

'You have lived there long?'

'Fourteen years.'

'And your household consists of you and your husband. Any children?'

'No.'

'But a niece, I think you said?'

'Yes, Freda Stanton, the child of my husband's only sister. She has lived with us for the last eight years – that is, until a week ago.'

'Oh, and what happened a week ago?'

'Things hadn't been very pleasant for some time; I don't know what had come over Freda. She was so rude and impertinent, and her temper something shocking, and in the end she flared up one day, and out she walked and took rooms of her own in the town. I've not seen her since. Better leave her to come to her senses, so Mr Radnor says.'

'Who is Mr Radnor?'

Some of Mrs Pengelley's initial embarrassment returned.

'Oh, he's – he's just a friend. Very pleasant young fellow.'

'Anything between him and your niece?'

'Nothing whatever,' said Mrs Pengelley emphatically.

Poirot shifted his ground.

'You and your husband are, I presume, in comfortable circumstances?'

'Yes, we're very nicely off.'

'The money, is it yours or your husband's?'

'Oh, it's all Edward's. I've nothing of my own.'

'You see, madame, to be businesslike, we must be brutal. We must seek for a motive. Your husband, he would not poison you just *pour passer le temps*! Do you know of any reason why he should wish you out of the way?'

'There's the yellow-haired hussy who works for him,' said Mrs Pengelley, with a flash of temper. 'My husband's a dentist, M. Poirot, and nothing would do but he must have a smart girl, as he said, with bobbed hair and a white overall, to make his appointments and mix his fillings for him. It's come to my ears that there have been fine goings-on, though of course he swears it's all right.'

'This bottle of weed-killer, madame, who ordered it?'

'My husband – about a year ago.'

'Your niece, now, has she any money of her own?'

'About fifty pounds a year, I should say. She'd be glad enough to come back and keep house for Edward if I left him.'

'You have contemplated leaving him, then?'

'I don't intend to let him have it all his own way. Women aren't the downtrodden slaves they were in the old days, M. Poirot.'

'I congratulate you on your independent spirit, madame; but let us be practical. You return to Polgarwith today?'

'Yes, I came up by an excursion. Six this morning the train started, and the train goes back at five this afternoon.'

'*Bien*! I have nothing of great moment on hand. I can devote myself to your little affair. Tomorrow I shall be in Polgarwith. Shall we say that Hastings, here, is a distant relative of yours, the son of your second cousin? Me, I am his eccentric foreign friend. In the meantime, eat only what is prepared by your own hands, or under your eye. You have a maid whom you trust?'

'Jessie is a very good girl, I am sure.'

'Till tomorrow then, madame, and be of good courage.'

Poirot bowed the lady out, and returned thoughtfully to his chair. His absorption was not so great, however, that he failed to see two minute strands of feather scarf wrenched off by the lady's agitated fingers. He collected them carefully and consigned them to the wastepaper basket.

'What do you make of the case, Hastings?'

'A nasty business, I should say.'

'Yes, if what the lady suspects be true. But is it? Woe betide any husband who orders a bottle of weed-killer nowadays. If his wife suffers from gastritis, and is inclined to be of a hysterical temperament, the fat is in the fire.'

'You think that is all there is to it?'

'Ah – *voilà* – I do not know, Hastings. But the case interests me – it interests me enormously. For, you see, it has positively no new features. Hence the hysterical theory, and yet Mrs Pengelley did not strike me as being a hysterical woman. Yes, if I mistake not, we have here a very poignant human drama. Tell me, Hastings, what do you consider Mrs Pengelley's feelings towards her husband to be?'

'Loyalty struggling with fear,' I suggested.

'Yet, ordinarily, a woman will accuse anyone in the world – but not her husband. She will stick to her belief in him through thick and thin.'

'The "other woman" complicates the matter.'

'Yes, affection may turn to hate, under the stimulus of jealousy. But hate would take her to the police – not to me. She would want an outcry – a scandal. No, no, let us exercise our little grey cells. Why did she come to me? To have her suspicions proved wrong? Or – to have them *proved right*? Ah, we have here something I do not understand – an unknown factor. Is she a superb actress, our Mrs Pengelley? No, she was genuine, I would swear that she was genuine, and therefore I am interested. Look up the trains to Polgarwith, I pray you.'

The best train of the day was the one-fifty from Paddington which reached Polgarwith just after seven o'clock. The journey was uneventful, and I had to rouse myself from a pleasant nap to alight upon the platform of the bleak little station. We took our bags to the Duchy Hotel, and after a light meal, Poirot suggested our stepping round to pay an after-dinner call on my so-called cousin.

The Pengelleys' house stood a little way back from the road with an old-fashioned cottage garden in front. The smell of stocks and mignonette came sweetly wafted on the evening breeze. It seemed impossible to associate thoughts of violence with this Old World charm. Poirot rang and knocked. As the summons was not answered, he rang again. This time, after a little pause, the door was opened by a dishevelled-looking servant. Her eyes were red, and she was sniffing violently.

'We wish to see Mrs Pengelley,' explained Poirot. 'May we enter?'

The maid stared. Then, with unusual directness, she

answered: 'Haven't you heard, then? She's dead. Died this evening – about half an hour ago.'

We stood staring at her, stunned.

'What did she die of?' I asked at last.

'There's some as could tell.' She gave a quick glance over her shoulder. 'If it wasn't that somebody ought to be in the house with the missus, I'd pack my box and go tonight. But I'll not leave her dead with no one to watch by her. It's not my place to say anything, and I'm not going to say anything – but everybody knows. It's all over the town. And if Mr Radnor don't write to the 'Ome Secretary, someone else will. The doctor may say what he likes. Didn't I see the master with my own eyes a-lifting down of the weed-killer from the shelf this very evening? And didn't he jump when he turned round and saw me watching of him? And the missus' gruel there on the table, all ready to take to her? Not another bit of food passes my lips while I am in this house Not if I dies for it.'

'Where does the doctor live who attended your mistress?'

'Dr Adams. Round the corner in High Street. The second house.'

Poirot turned away abruptly. He was very pale.

'For a girl who was not going to say anything, that girl said a lot,' I remarked dryly.

Poirot struck his clenched hand into his palm.

'An imbecile, a criminal imbecile, that is what I have been, Hastings. I have boasted of my little grey cells, and now I have lost a human life, a life that came to me to be saved. Never did I dream that anything would happen so soon. May the good God forgive me, but I never believed anything would happen at all. Her story seemed to me artificial. Here we are at the doctor's. Let us see what he can tell us.'

Dr Adams was the typical genial red-faced country doctor of fiction. He received us politely enough, but at a hint of our errand, his red face became purple.

'Damned nonsense Damned nonsense, every word of it Wasn't I in attendance on the case? Gastritis – gastritis pure and simple. This town's a hotbed of gossip – a lot of scandal-mongering old women get together and invent God known what. They read these scurrilous rags of newspapers, and nothing will suit them but that someone in their town shall get poisoned too. They see a bottle of weed-killer on a shelf – and hey presto! – away goes their imagination with the bit between his teeth. I know Edward Pengelley – he wouldn't poison his grandmother's dog. And why should he poison his wife? Tell me that?'

'There is one thing, M. le Docteur, that perhaps you do not know.'

And, very briefly, Poirot outlined the main facts of Mrs Pengelley's visit to him. No one could have been more astonished than Dr Adams. His eyes almost started out of his head.

'God bless my soul!' he ejaculated. 'The poor woman must have been mad. Why didn't she speak to me? That was the proper thing to do.'

'And have her fears ridiculed?'

'Not at all, not at all. I hope I've got an open mind.'

Poirot looked at him and smiled. The physician was evidently more perturbed than he cared to admit. As we left the house, Poirot broke into a laugh.

'He is as obstinate as a pig, that one. He has said it is gastritis; therefore it is gastritis! All the same, he has the mind uneasy.'

'What's our next step?'

'A return to the inn, and a night of horror upon one of your English provincial beds, *mon ami*. It is a thing to make pity, the cheap English bed!'

'And tomorrow?'

'*Rien à faire*. We must return to town and await developments.'

'That's very tame,' I said, disappointed. 'Suppose there are none?'

'There will be! I promise you that. Our old doctor may give as many certificates as he pleases. He cannot stop several hundred tongues from wagging. And they will wag to some purpose, I can tell you that!'

Our train for town left at eleven the following morning. Before we started for the station, Poirot expressed a wish to see Miss Freda Stanton, the niece mentioned to us by the dead woman. We found the house where she was lodging easily enough. With her was a tall, dark young man whom she introduced in some confusion as Mr Jacob Radnor.

Miss Freda Stanton was an extremely pretty girl of the old Cornish type – dark hair and eyes and rosy cheeks. There was a flash in those same dark eyes which told of a temper that it would not be wise to provoke.

'Poor Auntie,' she said, when Poirot had introduced himself, and explained his business. 'It's terribly sad. I've been wishing all the morning that I'd been kinder and more patient.'

'You stood a great deal, Freda,' interrupted Radnor.

'Yes, Jacob, but I've got a sharp temper, I know. After all, it was only silliness on Auntie's part. I ought to have just laughed and not minded. Of course, it's all nonsense her thinking that Uncle was poisoning her. She *was* worse after any food he gave her – but I'm sure it was only from thinking about it. She made up her mind she would be, and then she was.'

'What was the actual cause of your disagreement, *mademoiselle*?'

Miss Stanton hesitated, looking at Radnor. That young gentleman was quick to take the hint.

'I must be getting along, Freda. See you this evening. Goodbye, gentlemen; you're on your way to the station, I suppose?'

Poirot replied that we were, and Radnor departed.

'You are affianced, is it not so?' demanded Poirot, with a sly smile.

Freda Stanton blushed and admitted that such was the case.

'And that was really the whole trouble with Auntie,' she added.

'She did not approve of the match for you?'

'Oh, it wasn't that so much. But you see, she – ' The girl came to a stop.

'Yes?' encouraged Poirot gently.

'It seems rather a horrid thing to say about her – now she's dead. But you'll never understand unless I tell you. Auntie was absolutely infatuated with Jacob.'

'Indeed?'

'Yes, wasn't it absurd? She was over fifty, and he's not quite thirty! But there it was. She was silly about him! I had to tell her at last that it was me he was after – and she carried on dreadfully. She wouldn't believe a word of it, and was so rude and insulting that it's no wonder I lost my temper. I talked it over with Jacob, and we agreed that the best thing to do was for me to clear out for a bit till she came to her senses. Poor Auntie – I suppose she was in a queer state altogether.'

'It would certainly seem so. Thank you, mademoiselle, for making things so clear to me.'

A little to my surprise, Radnor was waiting for us in the street below.

'I can guess pretty well what Freda has been telling you,' he remarked. 'It was a most unfortunate thing to

happen, and very awkward for me, as you can imagine.
I need hardly say that it was none of my doing. I was
pleased at first, because I imagined the old woman was
helping on things with Freda. The whole thing was
absurd – but extremely unpleasant.'

'When are you and Miss Stanton going to be married?'

'Soon, I hope. Now, M. Poirot, I'm going to be candid
with you. I know a bit more than Freda does. She
believes her uncle to be innocent. I'm not so sure. But
I can tell you one thing: I'm going to keep my mouth
shut about what I do know. Let sleeping dogs lie. I don't
want my wife's uncle tried and hanged for murder.'

'Why do you tell me all this?'

'Because I've heard of you, and I know you're a clever
man. It's quite possible that you might ferret out a case
against him. But I put it to you – what good is that?
The poor woman is past help, and she'd have been the
last person to want a scandal – why, she'd turn in her
grave at the mere thought of it.'

'You are probably right there. You want me to – hush
it up, then?'

'That's my idea. I'll admit frankly that I'm selfish
about it. I've got my way to make – and I'm building
up a good little business as a tailor and outfitter.'

'Most of us are selfish, Mr Radnor. Not all of us admit
it so freely. I will do what you ask – but I tell you frankly
you will not succeed in hushing it up.'

'Why not?'

Poirot held up a finger. It was market day, and we
were passing the market – a busy hum came from within.

'The voice of the people – that is why, Mr Radnor.
Ah, we must run, or we shall miss our train.'

'Very interesting, is it not, Hastings?' said Poirot, as the
train steamed out of the station.

He had taken out a small comb from his pocket, also

17

a microscopic mirror, and was carefully arranging his moustache, the symmetry of which had become slightly impaired during our brisk run.

'You seem to find it so,' I replied. 'To me, it is all rather sordid and unpleasant. There's hardly any mystery about it.'

'I agree with you; there is no mystery whatever.'

'I suppose we can accept the girl's rather extraordinary story of her aunt's infatuation? That seemed the only fishy part to me. She was such a nice, respectable woman.'

'There is nothing extraordinary about that – it is completely ordinary. If you read the papers carefully, you will find that often a nice respectable woman of that age leaves a husband she has lived with for twenty years, and sometimes a whole family of children as well, in order to link her life with that of a young man considerably her junior. You admire *les femmes*, Hastings; you prostrate yourself before all of them who are good-looking and have the good taste to smile upon you; but psychologically you know nothing whatever about them. In the autumn of a woman's life, there comes always one mad moment when she longs for romance, for adventure – before it is too late. It comes none the less surely to a woman because she is the wife of a respectable dentist in a country town!'

'And you think – '

'That a clever man might take advantage of such a moment.'

'I shouldn't call Pengelley so clever,' I mused. 'He's got the whole town by the ears. And yet I suppose you're right. The only two men who know anything, Radnor and the doctor, both want to hush it up. He's managed that somehow. I wish we'd seen the fellow.'

'You can indulge your wish. Return by the next train and invent an aching molar.'

I looked at him keenly.

'I wish I knew what you considered so interesting about the case.'

'My interest is very aptly summed up by a remark of yours, Hastings. After interviewing the maid, you observed that for someone who was not going to say a word, she had said a good deal.'

'Oh!' I said doubtfully; then I harped back to my original criticism: 'I wonder why you made no attempt to see Pengelley?'

'*Mon ami*, I give him just three months. Then I shall see him for as long as I please – in the dock.'

For once I thought Poirot's prognostications were going to be proved wrong. The time went by, and nothing transpired as to our Cornish case. Other matters occupied us, and I had nearly forgotten the Pengelley tragedy when it was suddenly recalled to me by a short paragraph in the paper which stated that an order to exhume the body of Mrs Pengelley had been obtained from the Home Secretary.

A few days later, and 'The Cornish Mystery' was the topic of every paper. It seemed that gossip had never entirely died down, and when the engagement of the widower to Miss Marks, his secretary, was announced, the tongues burst out again louder than ever. Finally a petition was sent to the Home Secretary; the body was exhumed; large quantities of arsenic were discovered; and Mr Pengelley was arrested and charged with the murder of his wife.

Poirot and I attended the preliminary proceedings. The evidence was much as might have been expected. Dr Adams admitted that the symptoms of arsenical poisoning might easily be mistaken for those of gastritis. The Home Office expert gave his evidence; the maid Jessie poured out a flood of voluble information, most of which was rejected, but which certainly strengthened the case against the prisoner. Freda Stanton gave evidence as to her aunt's being worse whenever she ate food prepared by her husband. Jacob Radnor told how he had dropped in unexpectedly on the day of Mrs Pengelley's death, and found Pengelley replacing the bottle of weed-killer on the pantry shelf, Mrs Pengelley's gruel being on the table close by. Then Miss Marks, the fair-haired secretary, was called, and wept and went into hysterics and admitted that there had been 'passages' between her and her employer, and that he had promised to marry her in the event of anything happening to his wife. Pengelley reserved his defence and was sent for trial.

Jacob Radnor walked back with us to our lodgings.

'You see, Mr Radnor,' said Poirot, 'I was right. The voice of the people spoke – and with no uncertain voice. There was to be no hushing up of this case.'

'You were quite right,' sighed Radnor. 'Do you see any chance of his getting off?'

'Well, he has reserved his defence. He may have something – up the sleeves, as you English say. Come in with us, will you not?'

Radnor accepted the invitation. I ordered two whiskies and sodas and a cup of chocolate. The last order caused consternation, and I much doubted whether it would ever put in an appearance.

'Of course,' continued Poirot, 'I have a good deal of experience in matters of this kind. And I see only one loophole of escape for our friend.'

'What is it?'

'That you should sign this paper.'

With the suddenness of a conjuror, he produced a sheet of paper covered with writing.

'What is it?'

'A confession that you murdered Mrs Pengelley.'

There was a moment's pause; then Radnor laughed.

'You must be mad!'

'No, no, my friend, I am not mad. You came here; you started a little business; you were short of money. Mr Pengelley was a man very well-to-do. You met his niece; she was inclined to smile upon you. But the small allowance that Pengelley might have given her upon her marriage was not enough for you. You must get rid of both the uncle and the aunt; then the money would come to her, since she was the only relative. How cleverly you set about it! You made love to that plain middle-aged woman until she was your slave. You implanted in her doubts of her husband. She discovered first that he was deceiving her – then, under your guidance, that he was trying to poison her. You were often at the house; you had opportunities to introduce the arsenic into her food. But you were careful never to do so when her husband was away. Being a woman, she did not keep her suspicions to herself. She talked to her niece; doubtless she talked to other women friends. Your only difficulty was keeping up separate relations with the two women, and even that was not so difficult as it looked. You explained to the aunt that, to allay the suspicions of her husband, you had to pretend to pay court to the niece. And the younger lady needed little convincing – she would never seriously consider her aunt as a rival.

'But then Mrs Pengelley made up her mind, without saying anything to you, to consult *me*. If she could be really assured, beyond any possible doubt, that her husband was trying to poison her, she would feel justified in leaving him, and linking her life with yours – which is what she imagined you wanted her to do. But that did not suit your book at all. You did not want a detective prying around. A favourable minute occurs. You are in the house when Mr Pengelley is getting some gruel for his wife, and you introduce the fatal dose. The rest is easy. Apparently anxious to hush matters up, you secretly foment them. But you reckoned without Hercule Poirot, my intelligent young friend.'

Radnor was deadly pale, but he still endeavoured to carry off matters with a high hand.

'Very interesting and ingenious, but why tell me all this?'

'Because, monsieur, I represent – not the law, but Mrs Pengelley. For her sake, I give you a chance of escape. Sign this paper, and you shall have twenty-four hours' start – twenty-four hours before I place it in the hands of the police.'

Radnor hesitated.

'You can't prove anything.'

'Can't I? I am Hercule Poirot. Look out of the window, monsieur. There are two men in the street. They have orders not to lose sight of you.'

Radnor strode across to the window and pulled aside the blind, then shrank back with an oath.

'You see, monsieur? Sign – it is your best chance.'

'What guarantee have I – '

'That I shall keep faith? The word of Hercule Poirot. You will sign? Good. Hastings, be so kind as to pull that left-hand blind half-way up. That is the signal that Mr Radnor may leave unmolested.'

White, muttering oaths, Radnor hurried from the room.

Poirot nodded gently.

'A coward! I always knew it.'

'It seems to me, Poirot, that you've acted in a criminal manner,' I cried angrily. 'You always preach against sentiment. And here you are letting a dangerous criminal escape out of sheer sentimentality.'

'That was not sentiment – that was business,' replied Poirot. 'Do you not see, my friend, that we have no shadow of proof against him? Shall I get up and say to twelve stolid Cornishmen that I, Hercule Poirot, *know*? They would laugh at me. The only chance was to frighten him and get a confession that way. Those two loafers that I noticed outside came in very useful. Pull down the blind again, will you, Hastings. Not that there was any reason for raising it. It was part of our *mise en scéne*.

'Well, well, we must keep our word. Twenty-four hours, did I say? So much longer for poor Mr Pengelley – and it is not more than he deserves; for mark you, he deceived his wife. I am very strong on the family life, as you know. Ah, well, twenty-four hours – and then? I have great faith in Scotland Yard. They will get him, *mon ami;* they will get him.'

THE VEILED LADY

I had noticed that for some time Poirot had been growing increasingly dissatisfied and restless. We had had no interesting cases of late, nothing on which my little friend could exercise his keen wits and remarkable powers of deduction. This morning he flung down the newspaper with an impatient '*Tchah*' – a favourite exclamation of his which sounded exactly like a cat sneezing.

'They fear me, Hastings; the criminals of your England they fear me! When the cat is there, the little mice, they come no more to the cheese!'

'I don't suppose the greater part of them even know of your existence,' I said, laughing.

Poirot looked at me reproachfully. He always imagines that the whole world is thinking and talking of Hercule Poirot. He had certainly made a name for himself in London, but I could hardly believe that his existence struck terror into the criminal world.

'What about that daylight robbery of jewels in Bond Street the other day?' I asked.

'A neat *coup*,' said Poirot approvingly, 'though not in my line. *Pas de finesse, seulement de l'audace*! A man with a loaded cane smashes the plate-glass window of a jeweller's shop and grabs a number of precious stones. Worthy citizens immediately seize him; a policeman arrives. He is caught red-handed with the jewels on him. He is marched off to the police, and then it is discovered that the stones are paste. He has passed the real ones to a confederate – one of the aforementioned worthy citizens. He will go to prison – true; but when he comes out, there will be a nice little fortune awaiting him. Yes, not badly imagined. But I could do better than that. Sometimes, Hastings, I regret that I am of such a moral disposition. To work against the law, it would be pleasing, for a change.'

'Cheer up, Poirot; you know you are unique in your own line.'

'But what is there on hand in my own line?'

I picked up the paper.

'Here's an Englishman mysteriously done to death in Holland,' I said.

'They always say that – and later they find that he ate the tinned fish and that his death is perfectly natural.'

'Well, if you're determined to grouse!'

'*Tiens!*' said Poirot, who had strolled across to the window. 'Here in the street is what they call in novels a "heavily veiled lady". She mounts the steps; she rings the bell – she comes to consult us. Here is a possibility of something interesting. When one is as young and pretty as that one, one does not veil the face except for a big affair.'

A minute later our visitor was ushered in. As Poirot had said, she was indeed heavily veiled. It was impossible to distinguish her features until she raised her veil of black Spanish lace. Then I saw that Poirot's intuition had been right; the lady was extremely pretty, with fair hair and blue eyes. From the costly simplicity of her attire, I deduced at once that she belonged to the upper strata of society.

'Monsieur Poirot,' said the lady in a soft, musical voice, 'I am in great trouble. I can hardly believe that you can help me, but I have heard such wonderful things of you that I come literally as the last hope to beg you to do the impossible.'

'The impossible, it pleases me always,' said Poirot. 'Continue, I beg of you, mademoiselle.'

Our fair guest hesitated.

'But you must be frank,' added Poirot. 'You must not leave me in the dark on any point.'

'I will trust you,' said the girl suddenly. 'You have heard of Lady Millicent Castle Vaughan?'

I looked up with keen interest. The announcement of Lady Millicent's engagement to the young Duke of Southshire had appeared a few days previously. She was, I knew, the fifth daughter of an impecunious Irish peer, and the Duke of Southshire was one of the best matches in England.

'I am Lady Millicent,' continued the girl. 'You may have read of my engagement. I should be one of the happiest girls alive; but oh, M. Poirot, I am in terrible trouble! There is a man, a horrible man – his name is Lavington; and he – I hardly know how to tell you. There was a letter I wrote – I was only sixteen at the time; and he – he –'

'A letter that you wrote to this Mr Lavington?'

'Oh *no* – not to him! To a young soldier – I was very fond of him – he was killed in the war.'

'I understand,' said Poirot kindly.

'It was a foolish letter, an indiscreet letter, but indeed, M. Poirot, nothing more. But there are phrases in it which – which might bear a different interpretation.'

'I see,' said Poirot. 'And this letter has come into the possession of Mr Lavington?'

'Yes, and he threatens, unless I pay him an enormous sum of money, a sum that is quite impossible for me to raise, to send it to the Duke.'

'The dirty swine!' I ejaculated. 'I beg your pardon, Lady Millicent.'

'Would it not be wiser to confess all to your future husband?'

'I dare not, M. Poirot. The Duke is a rather peculiar character, jealous and suspicious and prone to believe the worst. I might as well break off my engagement at once.'

'Dear, dear,' said Poirot with an expressive grimace. 'And what do you want me to do, milady?'

'I thought perhaps that I might ask Mr Lavington to call upon you. I would tell him that you were empowered by me to discuss the matter. Perhaps you could reduce his demands.'

'What sum does he mention?'

'Twenty thousand pounds – an impossibility. I doubt if I could raise a thousand, even.'

'You might perhaps borrow the money on the prospect of your approaching marriage – but I doubt if you could get hold of half that sum. Besides – *eh bien*, it is repugnant to me that you should pay! No, the ingenuity of Hercule Poirot shall defeat your enemies! Send me this Mr Lavington. Is he likely to bring the letter with him?'

The girl shook her head.

'I do not think so. He is very cautious.'

'I suppose there is no doubt that he really has it?'

'He showed it to me when I went to his house.'

'You went to his house? That was very imprudent, milady.'

'Was it? I was so desperate. I hoped my entreaties might move him.'

'*Oh là là!* The Lavingtons of this world are not moved by entreaties! He would welcome them as showing how much importance you attached to the document. Where does he live, this fine gentleman?'

'At Buona Vista, Wimbledon. I went there after dark – '
Poirot groaned. 'I declared that I would inform the police in the end, but he only laughed in a horrid, sneering manner. "By all means, my dear Lady Millicent, do so if you wish," he said.

'Yes, it is hardly an affair for the police,' murmured Poirot.

' "But I think you will be wiser than that," he continued. "See, here is your letter – in this little Chinese puzzle box!" He held it so that I could see. I tried to snatch at it, but he was too quick for me. With a horrid smile he folded it up and replaced it in the little wooden box. "It will be quite safe here, I assure you," he said, "and the box itself lives in such a clever place that you would never find it." My eyes turned to the small wallsafe, and he shook his head and laughed. "I have a better safe than that," he said. Oh, he was odious! M. Poirot, do you think that you can help me?'

'Have faith in Papa Poirot. I will find a way.'

These reassurances were all very well, I thought, as Poirot gallantly ushered his fair client down the stairs, but it seemed to me that we had a tough nut to crack. I said as much to Poirot when he returned. He nodded ruefully.

'Yes – the solution does not leap to the eye. He has the whip hand, this M. Lavington. For the moment I do not see how we are to circumvent him.'

Mr Lavington duly called upon us that afternoon. Lady Millicent had spoken truly when she described him as an odious man. I felt a positive tingling in the end of my boot, so keen was I to kick him down the stairs. He was blustering and overbearing in manner, laughed Poirot's gentle suggestions to scorn, and generally showed himself as master of the situation. I could not help feeling that Poirot was hardly appearing at his best. He looked discouraged and crestfallen.

'Well, gentlemen,' said Lavington, as he took up his hat, 'we don't seem to be getting much further. The case stands like this: I'll let the Lady Millicent off cheap, as she is such a charming young lady.' He leered odiously. 'We'll say eighteen thousand. I'm off to Paris today – a little piece of business to attend to over there. I shall be back on Tuesday. Unless the money is paid by Tuesday evening, the letter goes to the Duke. Don't tell me Lady Millicent can't raise the money. Some of her gentlemen friends would be only too willing to oblige such a pretty woman with a loan – if she goes the right way about it.'

My face flushed, and I took a step forward, but Lavington had wheeled out of the room as he finished his sentence.

'My God!' I cried. 'Something has got to be done. You seem to be taking this lying down, Poirot.'

'You have an excellent heart, my friend – but your grey cells are in a deplorable condition. I have no wish to impress Mr Lavington with my capabilities. The more pusillanimous he thinks me, the better.'

'Why?'

'It is curious,' murmured Poirot reminiscently, 'that I should have uttered a wish to work against the law just before Lady Millicent arrived!'

'You are going to burgle his house while he is away?' I gasped.

'Sometimes, Hastings, your mental processes are amazingly quick.'

'Suppose he takes the letter with him?'

Poirot shook his head.

'That is very unlikely. He has evidently a hiding-place in his house that he fancies to be pretty impregnable.'

'When do we – er – do the deed?'

'Tomorow night. We will start from here about eleven o'clock.'

At the time appointed I was ready to set off. I had donned a dark suit, and a soft dark hat. Poirot beamed kindly on me.

'You have dressed the part, I see,' he observed. 'Come let us take the underground to Wimbledon.'

'Aren't we going to take anything with us? Tools to break in with?'

'My dear Hastings, Hercule Poirot does not adopt such crude methods.'

I retired, snubbed, but my curiosity was alert.

It was just on midnight that we entered the small suburban garden of Buona Vista. The house was dark and silent. Poirot went straight to a window at the back of the house, raised the sash noiselessly and bade me enter.

'How did you know this window would be open?' I whispered, for really it seemed uncanny.

'Because I sawed through the catch this morning.'

'What?'

'But yes, it was most simple. I called, presented a fictitious card and one of Inspector Japp's official ones. I said I had been sent, recommended by Scotland Yard, to attend to some burglar-proof fastenings that Mr Lavington wanted fixed while he was away. The housekeeper welcomed me with enthusiasm. It seems they have had two attempted burglaries here lately – evidently our little idea has occurred to other clients of Mr Lavington's – with nothing of value taken. I examined all the windows, made my little arrangement, forbade the servants to touch the windows until tomorrow, as they were electrically connected up, and withdrew gracefully.'

'Really, Poirot, you are wonderful.'

'*Mon ami*, it was of the simplest. Now, to work! The servants sleep at the top of the house, so we will run little risk of disturbing them.'

'I presume the safe is built into the wall somewhere?'

'Safe? Fiddlesticks! There is no safe. Mr Lavington is an intelligent man. You will see, he will have devised a hiding place much more intelligent than a safe. A safe is the first thing everyone looks for.'

Whereupon we began a systematic search of the entire place. But after several hours' ransacking of the house, our search had been unavailing. I saw symptoms of anger gathering on Poirot's face.

'*Ah sapristi*, is Hercule Poirot to be beaten? Never! Let us be calm. Let us reflect. Let us reason. Let us – *enfin!* – employ our little grey cells!'

He paused for some moments, bending his brows in concentration; then the green light I knew so well stole into his eyes.

'I have been an imbecile! The kitchen!'

'The kitchen,' I cried. 'But that's impossible. The servants!'

'Exactly. Just what ninety-nine people out of a hundred would say! And for that very reason the kitchen is the ideal place to choose. It is full of various homely objects. *En avant*, to the kitchen!'

I followed him, completely sceptical, and watched whilst he dived into bread-bins, tapped saucepans, and put his head into the gas vent. In the end, tired of watching him, I strolled back to the study. I was convinced that there, and there only, would we find the *cache*. I made a further minute search, noted that it was now a quarter past four and that therefore it would soon be growing light, and then went back to the kitchen regions.

To my utter amazement, Poirot was now standing right inside the coal-bin, to the utter ruin of his neat light suit. He made a grimace.

'But yes, my friend, it is against all my instincts so to ruin my appearance, but what will you?'

'But Lavington can't have buried it under the coal?'

'If you would use your eyes, you would see that it is not the coal that I examine.'

I then saw on a shelf behind the coal-bunker some logs of wood were piled. Poirot was dexterously taking them down one by one. Suddenly he uttered a low exclamation.

'Your knife, Hastings!'

I handed it to him. He appeared to insert it in the wood, and suddenly the log split in two. It had been neatly sawn in half and a cavity hollowed out in the centre. From this cavity Poirot took a little wooden box of Chinese make.

'Well done!' I cried, carried out of myself.

'Gently, Hastings! Do not raise your voice too much. Come, let us be off, before the daylight is upon us.'

Slipping the box into his pocket, he leaped lightly out of the coal-bunker, brushed himself down as well as he could, and leaving the house by the same way as we had come, we walked rapidly in the direction of London.

'But what an extraordinary place!' I expostulated. 'Anyone might have used the log.'

'In July, Hastings? And it was at the bottom of the pile – a very ingenious hiding-place. Ah, here is a taxi! Now for home, a wash, and a refreshing sleep.'

After the excitement of the night, I slept late. When I finally strolled into our sitting-room just before one o'clock, I was surprised to see Poirot, leaning back in an armchair, the Chinese box open beside him, calmly reading the letter he had taken from it.

He smiled at me affectionately, and tapped the sheet he held.

'She was right, the Lady Millicent; never would the Duke have pardoned this letter! It contains some of the most extravagant terms of affection I have ever come across.'

'Really, Poirot,' I said, rather disgustedly, 'I don't think you should have read the letter. That's the sort of thing that isn't done.'

'It is done by Hercule Poirot,' replied my friend imperturbably.

'And another thing,' I said. 'I don't think using Japp's official card yesterday was quite playing the game.'

'But I was not playing a game, Hastings. I was conducting a case.'

I shrugged my shoulders. One can't argue with a point of view.

'A step on the stairs,' said Poirot. 'That will be Lady Millicent.'

Our fair client came in with an anxious expression on her face which changed to one of delight on seeing the letter and box which Poirot held up.

'Oh, M. Poirot. How wonderful of you! How did you do it?'

'By rather reprehensible methods, milady. But Mr Lavington will not prosecute. This is your letter, is it not?'

She glanced through it.

'Yes. Oh, how can I ever thank you! You are a wonderful, wonderful man. Where was it hidden?'

Poirot told her.

'How very clever of you!' She took up the small box from the table. 'I shall keep this as a souvenir.'

'I had hoped, milady, that you would permit me to keep it – also as a souvenir.'

'I hope to send you a better souvenir than that – on my wedding-day. You shall not find me ungrateful, M. Poirot.'

'The pleasure of doing you a service will be more to me than a cheque – so you permit that I retain the box.'

'Oh no, M. Poirot, I simply must have that,' she cried laughingly.

She stretched out her hand, but Poirot was before her. His hand closed over it.

'I think not.' His voice had changed.

'What do you mean?' Her voice seemed to have grown sharper.

'At any rate, permit me to abstract its further contents. You observed that the original cavity has been reduced by half. In the top half, the compromising letter; in the bottom – '

He made a nimble gesture, then held out his hand. On the palm were four large glittering stones, and two big milky white pearls.

'The jewels stolen in Bond Street the other day, I rather fancy,' murmured Poirot. 'Japp will tell us.'

To my utter amazement, Japp himself stepped out from Poirot's bedroom.

'An old friend of yours, I believe,' said Poirot politely to Lady Millicent.

'Nabbed, by the Lord!' said Lady Millicent, with a complete change of manner. 'You nippy old devil!' She looked at Poirot with almost affectionate awe.

'Well, Gertie, my dear,' said Japp, 'the game's up this time, I fancy. Fancy seeing you again so soon! We've got your pal, too, the gentleman who called here the other day calling himself Lavington. As for Lavington himself, alias Croker, alias Reed, I wonder which of the gang it was who stuck a knife into him the other day in Holland? Thought he'd got the goods with him, didn't you? And he hadn't. He double-crossed you properly – hid 'em in his own house. You had two fellows looking for them, and then you tackled M. Poirot here, and by a piece of amazing luck he found them.'

'You do like talking, don't you?' said the late Lady Millicent. 'Easy there, now. I'll go quietly. You can't say that I'm not the perfect lady. Ta-ta, all!'

'The shoes were wrong,' said Poirot dreamily, while I was still too stupefied to speak. 'I have made my little observations of your English nation, and a lady, a born lady, is always particular about her shoes. She may have shabby clothes, but she will be well shod. Now, this Lady Millicent had smart, expensive clothes, and cheap shoes. It was not likely that either you or I should have seen the real Lady Millicent; she has been very little in London, and this girl had a certain superficial resemblance which would pass well enough. As I say, the shoes first awakened my suspicions, and then her story – and her veil – were a little melodramatic, eh? The Chinese box with a bogus compromising letter in the top must have been known to all the gang, but the log of wood was the late Mr Lavington's idea. *Eh, par exemple,* Hastings, I hope you will not again wound my feelings as you did yesterday by saying that I am unknown to the criminal classes. *Ma foi,* they even employ me when they themselves fail!'

DOUBLE SIN

I had called in at my friend Poirot's rooms to find him sadly overworked. So much had he become the rage that every rich woman who had mislaid a bracelet or lost a pet kitten rushed to secure the services of the great Hercule Poirot. My little friend was a strange mixture of Flemish thrift and artistic fervour. He accepted many cases in which he had little interest owing to the first instinct being predominant.

He also undertook cases in which there was a little or no monetary reward sheerly because the problem involved interested him. The result was that, as I say, he was overworking himself. He admitted as much himself, and I found little difficulty in persuading him to accompany me for a week's holiday to that well-known South Coast resort, Ebermouth.

We had spent four very agreeable days when Poirot came to me, an open letter in his hand.

'*Mon ami*, you remember my friend Joseph Aarons, the theatrical agent?'

I assented after a moment's thought. Poirot's friends are so many and so varied, and range from dustmen to dukes.

'*Eh bien*, Hastings, Joseph Aarons finds himself at Charlock Bay. He is far from well, and there is a little affair that it seems is worrying him. He begs me to go over and see him. I think, *mon ami*, that I must accede to his request. He is a faithful friend, the good Joseph Aarons, and has done much to assist me in the past.'

'Certainly, if you think so,' I said. 'I believe Charlock

Bay is a beautiful spot, and as it happens I've never been there.'

'Then we combine business with pleasure,' said Poirot. 'You will inquire the trains, yes?'

'It will probably mean a change or two,' I said with a grimace. 'You know what these cross-country lines are. To go from the South Devon Coast to the North Devon coast is sometimes a day's journey.'

However, on inquiry, I found that the journey could be accomplished by only one change at Exeter and that the trains were good. I was hastening back to Poirot with the information when I happened to pass the offices of the Speedy cars and saw written up:

Tomorrow. All-day excursion to Charlock Bay. Starting 8.30 through some of the most beautiful scenery in Devon.

I inquired a few particulars and returned to the hotel full of enthusiasm. Unfortunately, I found it hard to make Poirot share my feelings.

'My friend, why this passion for the motor coach? The train, see you, it is true? The tyres, they do not burst; the accidents, they do not happen. One is not incommoded by too much air. The windows can be shut and no draughts admitted.'

I hinted delicately that the advantage of fresh air was what attracted me most to the motor-coach scheme.

'And if it rains? Your English climate is so uncertain.'

'There's a hood and all that. Besides, if it rains badly, the excursion doesn't take place.'

'Ah!' said Poirot. 'Then let us hope that it rains.'

'Of course, if you feel like that and . . . '

'No, no, *mon ami*. I see that you have set your heart on the trip. Fortunately, I have my greatcoat with me

37

and two mufflers.' He sighed. 'But shall we have sufficient time at Charlock Bay?'

'Well, I'm afraid it means staying the night there. You see, the tour goes round by Dartmoor. We have lunch at Monkhampton. We arrive at Charlock Bay about four o'clock, and the coach starts back at five, arriving here at ten o'clock.'

'So!' said Poirot. 'And there are people who do this for pleasure! We shall, of course, get a reduction of the fare since we do not make the return journey?'

'I hardly think that's likely.'

'You must insist.'

'Come now, Poirot, don't be mean. You know you're coining money.'

'My friend, it is not the meanness. It is the business sense. If I were a millionaire, I would pay only what was just and right.'

As I had foreseen, however, Poirot was doomed to fail in this respect. The gentleman who issued tickets at the Speedy office was calm and unimpassioned but adamant. His point was that we ought to return. He even implied that we ought to pay extra for the privilege of leaving the coach at Charlock Bay.

Defeated, Poirot paid over the required sum and left the office.

'The English, they have no sense of money,' he grumbled. 'Did you observe a young man, Hastings, who paid over the full fare and yet mentioned his intention of leaving the coach at Monkhampton?'

'I don't think I did. As a matter of fact . . . '

'You were observing the pretty young lady who booked No. 5, the next seat to ours. Ah! Yes, my friend, I saw you. And that is why when I was on the point of taking seats No. 13 and 14 which are in the middle and as well sheltered as it is possible to be – you rudely pushed yourself forward and said that 3 and 4 would be better.'

'Really, Poirot,' I said, blushing.

'Auburn hair – always the auburn hair!'

'At any rate, she was more worth looking at than an odd young man.'

'That depends upon the point of view. To me, the young man was interesting.'

Something rather significant in Poirot's tone made me look at him quickly. 'Why? What do you mean?'

'Oh, do not excite yourself. Shall I say that he interested me because he was trying to grow a moustache and as yet the result is poor.' Poirot stroked his own magnificent moustache tenderly. 'It is an art,' he murmured, 'the growing of the moustache! I have sympathy for all who attempt it.'

It is always difficult with Poirot to know when he is serious and when he is merely amusing himself at one's expense. I judged it safest to say no more.

The following morning dawned bright and sunny. A really glorious day! Poirot, however, was taking no chances. He wore a woolly waistcoat, a mackintosh, a heavy overcoat, and two mufflers, in addition to wearing his thickest suit. He also swallowed two tablets of 'Antigrippe' before starting and packed a further supply.

We took a couple of small suitcases with us. The pretty girl we had noticed the day before had a small suitcase, and so did the young man whom I gathered to have been the object of Poirot's sympathy. Otherwise, there was no luggage. The four pieces were stowed away by the driver, and we all took our places.

Poirot, rather maliciously, I thought, assigned me the outside place as 'I had the mania for the fresh air' and himself occupied the seat next to our fair neighbour. Presently, however, he made amends. The man in seat 6 was a noisy fellow, inclined to be facetious and boisterous, and Poirot asked the girl in a low voice if she would like to change seats with him. She agreed gratefully, and the change having been effected, she entered into conversation with us and we were soon all three chattering together merrily.

She was evidently quite young, not more than nineteen, and as ingenuous as a child. She soon confided to us the reason for her trip. She was going, it seemed, on business for her aunt who kept a most interesting antique shop in Ebermouth.

This aunt had been left in very reduced circumstances on the death of her father and had used her small capital and a houseful of beautiful things which her father had left her to start in business. She had been extremely successful and had made quite a name for herself in the trade. This girl, Mary Durrant, had come to be with her aunt and learn the business and was very excited about it – much preferring it to the other alternative – becoming a nursery governess or companion.

Poirot nodded interest and approval to all this.

'Mademoiselle will be successful, I am sure,' he said gallantly. 'But I will give her a little word of advice. Do not be too trusting, mademoiselle. Everywhere in the world there are rogues and vagabonds, even it may be on this very coach of ours. One should always be on the guard, suspicious!'

She stared at him open-mouthed, and he nodded sapiently.

'But yes, it is as I say. Who knows? Even I who speak to you may be a malefactor of the worst description.'

And he twinkled more than ever at her surprised face.

We stopped for lunch at Monkhampton, and, after a few words with the waiter, Poirot managed to secure us a small table for three close by the window. Outside, in a big courtyard, about twenty char-a-bancs were parked – char-a-bancs which had come from all over the country.

The hotel dining-room was full, and the noise was rather considerable.

'One can have altogether too much of the holiday spirit,' I said with a grimace.

Mary Durrant agreed. 'Ebermouth is quite spoiled in the summers nowadays. My aunt says it used to be quite different. Now one can hardly get along the pavements for the crowd.'

'But it is good for business, mademoiselle.'

'Not for ours particularly. We sen only rare and valuable things. We do not go in for cheap bric-a-brac. My aunt has clients all over England. If they want a particular period table or chair, or a certain piece of china, they write to her, and, sooner or later, she gets it for them. That is what has happened in this case.'

We looked interested and she went on to explain. A certain American gentleman, Mr J. Baker Wood, was a connoisseur and collector of miniatures. A very valuable set of miniatures had recently come into the market, and Miss Elizabeth Penn – Mary's aunt – had purchased them. She had written to Mr Wood describing the miniatures and naming a price. He had replied at once, saying that he was prepared to purchase if the miniatures were as represented and asking that someone should be sent with them for him to see where he was staying at Charlock Bay. Miss Durrant had accordingly been despatched, acting as representative for the firm.

'They're lovely things, of course,' she said. 'But I can't imagine anyone paying all that money for them. Five hundred pounds! Just think of it! They're by Cosway. Is it Cosway I mean? I get so mixed up in these things.'

Poirot smiled. 'You are not yet experienced, eh, mademoiselle?'

'I've had no training,' said Mary ruefully. 'We weren't brought up to know about old things. It's a lot to learn.'

She sighed. Then suddenly, I saw her eyes widen in surprise. She was sitting facing the window, and her glance now was directed out of that window, into the courtyard. With a hurried word, she rose from her seat and almost ran out of the room. She returned in a few moments, breathless and apologetic.

'I'm so sorry rushing off like that. But I thought I saw a man taking my suitcase out of the coach. I went flying after him, and it turned out to be his own. It's one almost exactly like mine. I felt like such a fool. It looked as though I were accusing him of stealing it.'

She laughed at the idea.

Poirot, however, did not laugh. 'What man was it, mademoiselle? Describe him to me.'

'He had on a brown suit. A thin weedy young man with a very indeterminate moustache.'

'Aha,' said Poirot. 'Our friend of yesterday, Hastings. You know this young man, mademoiselle? You have seen him before?'

'No, never. Why?'

'Nothing. It is rather curious – that is all.'

He relapsed into silence and took no further part in the conversation until something Mary Durrant said caught his attention.

'Eh, mademoiselle, what is that you say?'

'I said that on my return journey I should have to be careful of "malefactors", as you call them. I believe Mr Wood always pays for things in cash. If I have five hundred pounds in notes on me, I shall be worth some malefactor's attention.'

She laughed but Poirot did not respond. Instead, he asked her what hotel she proposed to stay at in Charlock Bay.

'The Anchor Hotel. It is small and not expensive, but quite good.'

'So!' said Poirot. 'The Anchor Hotel. Precisely where Hastings here has made up his mind to stay. How odd!'

He twinkled at me.

'You are staying long in Charlock Bay?' asked Mary.

'One night only. I have business there. You could not guess, I am sure, what my profession is, mademoiselle?'

I saw Mary consider several possibilities and reject them – probably from a feeling of caution. At last, she hazarded the suggestion that Poirot was a conjurer. He was vastly entertained.

'Ah! But it is an idea that! You think I take the rabbits out of the hat? No, mademoiselle. Me, I am the opposite of a conjurer. The conjurer, he makes things disappear. Me, I make things that have disappeared, reappear.' He leaned forward dramatically so as to give the words full effect. 'It is a secret, mademoiselle, but I will tell you, I am a detective!'

He leaned back in his chair pleased with the effect he had created. Mary Durrant stared at him spellbound. But any further conversation was barred for the braying of various horns outside announced that the road monsters were ready to proceed.

As Poirot and I went out together I commented on the charm of our luncheon companion. Poirot agreed.

'Yes, she is charming. But, also rather silly?'

'Silly?'

'Do not be outraged. A girl may be beautiful and have auburn hair and yet be silly. It is the height of foolishness to take two strangers into her confidence as she has done.'

'Well, she could see we were all right.'

'That is imbecile, what you say, my friend. Anyone who knows his job – naturally he will appear "all right". That little one she talked of being careful when she would have five hundred pounds in money with her. But she has five hundred pounds with her now.'

'In miniatures.'

'Exactly. In miniatures. And between one and the other, there is no great difference, *mon ami.*'

'But no one knew about them except us.'

'And the waiter and the people at the next table. And, doubtless, several people in Ebermouth! Mademoiselle Durrant, she is charming, but, if I were Miss Elizabeth Penn, I would first of all instruct my new assistant in the common sense.' He paused and then said in a different voice: 'You know, my friend, it would be the easiest thing in the world to remove a suitcase from one of those char-a-bancs while we were all at luncheon.'

'Oh, come, Poirot, somebody will be sure to see.'

'And what would they see? Somebody removing his luggage. It would be done in an open and aboveboard manner, and it would be nobody's business to interfere.'

'Do you mean – Poirot, are you hinting – But that fellow in the brown suit – it was his own suitcase?'

Poirot frowned. 'So it seems. All the same, it is curious, Hastings, that he should have not removed his suitcase before, when the car first arrived. He has not lunched here, you notice.'

'If Miss Durrant hadn't been sitting opposite the window, she wouldn't have seen him,' I said slowly.

'And since it was his own suitcase, that would not have mattered,' said Poirot. 'So let us dismiss it from our thoughts, *mon ami.*'

Nevertheless, when we had resumed our places and were speeding along once more, he took the opportunity of giving Mary Durrant a further lecture on the dangers of indiscretion which she received meekly enough but with the air of thinking it all rather a joke.

We arrived at Charlock Bay at four o'clock and were fortunate enough to be able to get rooms at the Anchor Hotel – a charming old-world inn in one of the side streets.

Poirot had just unpacked a few necessaries and was applying a little cosmetic to his moustache preparatory to going out to call upon Joseph Aarons when there came a frenzied knocking at the door. I called 'Come in,' and, to my utter amazement, Mary Durrant appeared, her face white and large tears standing in her eyes.

'I do beg your pardon – but – but the most awful thing has happened. And you did say you were a detective?' This to Poirot.

'What has happened, mademoiselle?'

'I opened my suitcase. The miniatures were in a crocodile despatch case – locked, of course. Now, look!'

She held out a small square crocodile-covered case. The lid hung loose. Poirot took it from her. The case had been forced; great strength must have been used. The marks were plain enough. Poirot examined it and nodded.

'The miniatures?' he asked, though we both knew the answer well enough.

'Gone. They've been stolen. Oh, what shall I do?'

'Don't worry,' I said. 'My friend is Hercule Poirot. You must have heard of him. He'll get them back for you if anyone can.'

'Monsieur Poirot. The great Monsieur Poirot.'

Poirot was vain enough to be pleased at the obvious reverence in her voice. 'Yes, my child,' he said. 'It is I, myself. And you can leave your little affair in my hands. I will do all that can be done. But I fear – I much fear – that it will be too late. Tell me, was the lock of your suitcase forced also?'

She shook her head.

'Let me see it, please.'

We went together to her room, and Poirot examined the suitcase closely. It had obviously been opened with a key.

'Which is simple enough. These suitcase locks are all

45

much of the same pattern. *Eh bien*, we must ring up the police and we must also get in touch with Mr Baker Wood as soon as possible. I will attend to that myself.'

I went with him and asked what he meant by saying it might be too late. '*Mon cher*, I said today that I was the opposite of the conjurer – that I make the disappearing things reappear – but suppose someone has been before hand with me. You do not understand? You will in a minute.'

He disappeared into the telephone box. He came out five minutes later looking very grave. 'It is as I feared. A lady called upon Mr Wood with the miniatures half an hour ago. She represented herself as coming from Miss Elizabeth Penn. He was delighted with the miniatures and paid for them forthwith.'

'Half an hour ago – before we arrived here.'

Poirot smiled rather enigmatically. 'The Speedy cars are quite speedy, but a fast motor from, say, Monkhampton would get here a good hour ahead of them at least.'

'And what do we do now?'

'The good Hastings – always practical. We inform the police, do all we can for Miss Durrant, and – yes, I think decidedly, we have an interview with Mr J. Baker Wood.'

We carried out this programme. Poor Mary Durrant was terribly upset, fearing her aunt would blame her.

'Which she probably will,' observed Poirot, as we set out for the Seaside Hotel where Mr Wood was staying. 'And with perfect justice. The idea of leaving five hundred pounds' worth of valuables in a suitcase and going to lunch! All the same, *mon ami*, there are one or two curious points about the case. That despatch box, for instance, why was it forced?'

'To get out the miniatures.'

'But was not that a foolishness? Say our thief is tampering with the luggage at lunch-time under the pretext of getting out his own. Surely it is much simpler to open the suitcase, transfer the despatch case unopened to his own suitcase, and get away, than to waste the time forcing the lock?'

'He had to make sure the miniatures were inside.'

Poirot did not look convinced, but, as we were just being shown into Mr Wood's suite, we had no time for more discussion.

I took an immediate dislike to Mr Baker Wood.

He was a large vulgar man, very much overdressed and wearing a diamond solitaire ring. He was blustering and noisy.

Of course, he'd not suspected anything amiss. Why should he? The woman said she had the miniatures all right. Very fine specimens, too! Had he the numbers of the notes? No, he hadn't. And who was Mr – er – Poirot, anyway, to come asking him all these questions?

'I will not ask you anything more, monsieur, except for one thing. A description of the woman who called upon you. Was she young and pretty?'

'No, sir, she was not. Most emphatically not. A tall woman, middle-aged, grey hair, blotchy complexion and a budding moustache. A siren? Not on your life.'

'Poirot,' I cried, as we took our departure. 'A moustache. Did you hear?'

'I have the use of my ears, thank you, Hastings!'

'But what a very unpleasant man.'

'He has not the charming manner, no.'

'Well, we ought to get the thief all right,' I remarked. 'We can identify him.'

'You are of such a naïve simplicity, Hastings. Do you not know that there is such a thing as an alibi?'

'You think he will have an alibi?'

Poirot replied unexpectedly: 'I sincerely hope so.'

'The trouble with you is,' I said, 'that you like a thing to be difficult.'

'Quite right, *mon ami*. I do not like – how do you say it – the bird who sits!'

Poirot's prophecy was fully justified. Our travelling companion in the brown suit turned out to be a Mr Norton Kane. He had gone straight to the George Hotel at Monkhampton and had been there during the afternoon. The only evidence against him was that of Miss Durrant who declared that she had seen him getting out his luggage from the car while we were at lunch.

'Which in itself is not a suspicious act,' said Poirot meditatively.

After that remark, he lapsed into silence and refused to discuss the matter any further, saying when I pressed him, that he was thinking of moustaches in general, and that I should be well advised to do the same.

I discovered, however, that he had asked Joseph Aarons – with whom he spent the evening – to give him every detail possible about Mr Baker Wood. As both men were staying at the same hotel, there was a chance of gleaning some stray crumbs of information. Whatever Poirot learned, he kept to himself, however.

Mary Durrant, after various interviews with the police, had returned to Ebermouth by an early morning train. We lunched with Joseph Aarons, and after lunch, Poirot announced to me that he had settled the theatrical agent's problem satisfactorily, and that we could return to Ebermouth as soon as we liked. 'But not by road, *mon ami*; we go by rail this time.'

'Are you afraid of having your pocket picked, or of meeting another damsel in distress?'

'Both those affairs, Hastings, might happen to me on the train. No, I am in haste to be back in Ebermouth, because I want to proceed with our case.'

'Our case?'

'But, yes, my friend. Mademoiselle Durrant appealed to me to help her. Because the matter is now in the hands of the police, it does not follow that I am free to wash my hands of it. I came here to oblige an old friend, but it shall never be said of Hercule Poirot that he deserted a stranger in need!' And he drew himself up grandiloquently.

'I think you were interested before that,' I said shrewdly. 'In the office of cars, when you first caught sight of that young man, though what drew your attention to him I don't know.'

'Don't you, Hastings? You should. Well, well, that must remain my little secret.'

We had a short conversation with the police inspector in charge of the case before leaving. He had interviewed Mr Norton Kane, and told Poirot in confidence that the young man's manner had not impressed him favourably. He had blustered, denied, and contradicted himself.

'But just how the trick was done, I don't know,' he confessed. 'He could have handed the stuff to a confederate who pushed off at once in a fast car. But that's just theory. We've got to find the car and the confederate and pin the thing down.'

Poirot nodded thoughtfully.

'Do you think that was how it was done?' I asked him, as we were seated in the train.

'No, my friend, that was not how it was done. It was cleverer than that.'

'Won't you tell me?'

'Not yet. You know – it is my weakness – I like to keep my little secrets till the end.'

'Is the end going to be soon?'

'Very soon now.'

We arrived in Ebermouth a little after six and Poirot drove at once to the shop which bore the name 'Elizabeth Penn'. The establishment was closed, but Poirot rang the bell, and presently Mary herself opened the door, and expressed surprise and delight at seeing us.

'Please come in and see my aunt,' she said.

She led us into a back room. An elderly lady came forward to meet us; she had white hair and looked rather like a miniature herself with her pink-and-white skin and her blue eyes. Round her rather bent shoulders she wore a cape of priceless old lace.

'Is this the great Monsieur Poirot?' she asked in a low charming voice. 'Mary has been telling me. I could hardly believe it. And you will really help us in our trouble. You will advise us?'

Poirot looked at her for a moment, then bowed.

'Mademoiselle Penn – the effect is charming. But you should really grow a moustache.'

Miss Penn gave a gasp and drew back.

'You were absent from business yesterday, were you not?'

'I was here in the morning. Later I had a bad headache and went directly home.'

'Not home, mademoiselle. For your headache you tried the change of air, did you not? The air of Charlock Bay is very bracing, I believe.'

He took me by the arm and drew me towards the door. He paused there and spoke over his shoulder.

'You comprehend, I know everything. This little – farce – it must cease.'

There was a menace in his tone. Miss Penn, her face ghastly white, nodded mutely. Poirot turned to the girl.

'Mademoiselle,' he said gently, 'you are young and charming. But participating in these little affairs will lead to that youth and charm being hidden behind prison walls – and I, Hercule Poirot, tell you that that will be a pity.'

Then he stepped out into the street and I followed him, bewildered.

'From the first, *mon ami*, I was interested. When that young man booked his place as far as Monkhampton only, I saw the girl's attention suddenly riveted on him. Now why? He was not of the type to make a woman look at him for himself alone. When we started on the coach, I had a feeling that something would happen. Who saw the young man tampering with the luggage? Mademoiselle and mademoiselle only, and remember she chose that seat – a seat facing the window – a most unfeminine choice.

'And then she comes to us with the tale of robbery – the despatch box forced which makes not the common sense, as I told you at the time.

'And what is the result of it all? Mr Baker Wood has paid over good money for stolen goods. The miniatures will be returned to Miss Penn. She will sell them and will have made a thousand pounds instead of five hundred. I make the discreet inquiries and learn that her business is in a bad state – touch and go. I say to myself – the aunt and niece are in this together.'

'Then you never suspected Norton Kane?'

'*Mon ami*! With that moustache? A criminal is either clean shaven or he has a proper moustache that can be removed at will. But what an opportunity for the clever Miss Penn – a shrinking elderly lady with a pink-and-white complexion as we saw her. But if she holds herself erect, wears large boots, alters her complexion with a few unseemly blotches and – crowning touch – adds a few sparse hairs to her upper lip. What then? A masculine woman, says Mr Wood and "a man in disguise" say we at once.'

'She really went to Charlock yesterday?'

'Assuredly. The train, as you may remember telling me, left here at eleven and got to Charlock Bay at two o'clock. Then the return train is even quicker – the one we came by. It leaves Charlock at four-five and gets here at six-fifteen. Naturally, the miniatures were never in the despatch case at all. That was artistically forced before being packed. Mademoiselle Mary has only to find a couple of mugs who will be sympathetic to her charm and champion beauty in distress. But one of the mugs was no mug – he was Hercule Poirot!'

I hardly liked the inference. I said hurriedly: 'Then when you said you were helping a stranger, you were wilfully deceiving me. That's exactly what you were doing.'

'Never do I deceive you, Hastings. I only permit you to deceive yourself. I was referring to Mr Baker Wood – a stranger to these shores.' His face darkened. 'Ah! When I think of that imposition, that iniquitous overcharge, the same fare single to Charlock as return, my blood boils to protect the visitor! Not a pleasant man, Mr Baker Wood, not, as you would say, sympathetic. But a visitor! And we visitors, Hastings, must stand together. Me, I am all for the visitors!'

THE ADVENTURE OF 'THE WESTERN STAR'

I was standing at the window of Poirot's rooms looking out idly on the street below.

'That's queer,' I ejaculated suddenly beneath my breath.

'What is, *mon ami*?' asked Poirot placidly, from the depths of his comfortable chair.

'Deduce, Poirot, from the following facts! Here is a young lady, richly dressed – fashionable hat, magnificent furs. She is coming along slowly, looking up at the houses as she goes. Unknown to her, she is being shadowed by three men and a middle-aged woman. They have just been joined by an errand boy who points after the girl, gesticulating as he does so. What drama is this being played? Is the girl a crook, and are the shadowers detectives preparing to arrest her? Or are *they* the scoundrels, and are they plotting to attack an innocent victim? What does the great detective say?'

'The great detective, *mon ami*, chooses, as ever, the simplest course. He rises to see for himself.' And my friend joined me at the window.

In a minute he gave vent to an amused chuckle.

'As usual, your facts are tinged with your incurable romanticism. This is Miss Mary Marvell, the film star. She is being followed by a bevy of admirers who have recognized her. And, *en passant*, my dear Hastings, she is quite aware of the fact!'

I laughed.

'So all is explained. But you get no marks for that, Poirot. It was a mere matter of recognition.'

'*En vérité!* And how many times have you seen Mary Marvell on the screen, *mon cher*?'

I thought.

'About a dozen times perhaps.'

'And I – once! Yet *I* recognize her, and *you* do not.'

'She looks so different,' I replied rather feebly.

'Ah! *Sacré!*' cried Poirot. 'Is it that you expect her to promenade herself in the streets of London in a cowboy hat, or with bare feet, and a bunch of curls, as an Irish colleen? Always with you it is the non-essentials! Remember the case of the dancer, Valerie Saintclair.'

I shrugged my shoulders, slightly annoyed.

'But console yourself, *mon ami*,' said Poirot, calming down. 'All cannot be as Hercule Poirot! I know it well.'

'You really have the best opinion of yourself of anyone I ever knew!' I cried, divided between amusement and annoyance.

'What will you? When one is unique, one knows it! And others share that opinion – even, if I mistake it not, Miss Mary Marvell.'

'What?'

'Without doubt. She is coming here.'

'How do you make that out?'

'Very simply. This street, it is not aristocratic, *mon ami*! In it there is no fashionable doctor, no fashionable dentist – still less is there a fashionable milliner! But there *is* a fashionable detective. *Oui*, my friend, it is true – I am become the mode, the *dernier cri*! One says to another: "*Comment?* You have lost your gold pencil-case? You must go to the little Belgian. He is too marvellous! Everyone goes! *Courez!*" And they arrive! In flocks, *mon ami*! With problems of the most foolish!' A bell rang below. 'What did I tell you? That is Miss Marvell.'

As usual, Poirot was right. After a short interval, the

American film star was ushered in, and we rose to our feet.

Mary Marvell was undoubtedly one of the most popular actresses on the screen. She had only lately arrived in England in company with her husband, Gregory B. Rolf, also a film actor. Their marriage had taken place about a year ago in the States and this was their first visit to England. They had been given a great reception. Everyone was prepared to go mad over Mary Marvell, her wonderful clothes, her furs, her jewels, above all one jewel, the great diamond which had been nicknamed, to match its owner, 'the Western Star'. Much, true and untrue, had been written about this famous stone which was reported to be insured for the enormous sum of fifty thousand pounds.

All these details passed rapidly through my mind as I joined with Poirot in greeting our fair client.

Miss Marvell was small and slender, very fair and girlish looking, with the wide innocent blue eyes of a child.

Poirot drew forward a chair for her, and she commenced talking at once.

'You will probably think me very foolish, Monsieur Poirot, but Lord Cronshaw was telling me last night how wonderfully you cleared up the mystery of his nephew's death, and I felt that I just must have your advice. I dare say it's only a silly hoax – Gregory says so – but it's just worrying me to death.'

She paused for breath. Poirot beamed encouragement.

'Proceed, madame. You comprehend, I am still in the dark.'

'It's these letters.' Miss Marvell unclasped her handbag, and drew out three envelopes which she handed to Poirot.

The latter scrutinized them closely.

'Cheap paper – the name and address carefully

55

printed. Let us see the inside.' He drew out the enclosure.

I had joined him, and was leaning over his shoulder. The writing consisted of a single sentence, carefully printed like the envelope. It ran as follows:

'The great diamond which is the left eye of the god must return whence it came.'

The second letter was couched in precisely the same terms, but the third was more explicit:

'You have been warned. You have not obeyed. Now the diamond will be taken from you. At the full of the moon, the two diamonds which are the left and right eye of the god shall return. So it is written.'

'The first letter I treated as a joke,' explained Miss Marvell. 'When I got the second, I began to wonder. The third one came yesterday, and it seemed to me that, after all, the matter might be more serious than I had imagined.'

'I see they did not come by post, these letters.'

'No; they were left by hand – by a *Chinaman*. This is what frightens me.'

'Why?'

'Because it was from a Chink in San Francisco that Gregory bought the stone three years ago.'

'I see, madame, that you believe the diamond referred to to be – '

' "The Western Star",' finished Miss Marvell. 'That's so. At the time, Gregory remembers that there was some story attached to the stone, but the Chink wasn't handing out any information. Gregory says he seemed just scared to death, and in a mortal hurry to get rid of the thing.

He only asked about a tenth of its value. It was Greg's wedding present to me.'

Poirot nodded thoughtfully.

'The story seems of an almost unbelievable romanticism. And yet – who knows? I pray of you, Hastings, hand me my little almanac.'

I complied.

'*Voyons!*' said Poirot, turning the leaves. 'When is the date of the full moon? Ah, Friday next. That is in three days' time. *Eh bien*, madame, you seek my advice – I give it to you. This *belle histoire* may be a hoax – but it may not! Therefore I counsel you to place the diamond in my keeping until after Friday next. Then we can take what steps we please.'

A slight cloud passed over the actress's face, and she replied constrainedly:

'I'm afraid that's impossible.'

'You have it with you – *hein?*' Poirot was watching her narrowly.

The girl hesitated a moment, then slipped her hand into the bosom of her gown, drawing out a long thin chain. She leaned forward, unclosing her hand. In the palm, a stone of white fire, exquisitely set in platinum, lay and winked at us solemnly.

Poirot drew in his breath with a long hiss.

'*Épatant!*' he murmured. 'You permit, madame?' He took the jewel in his own hand and scrutinized it keenly, then restored it to her with a little bow. 'A magnificent stone – without a flaw. Ah, *cent tonnerres!* and you carry it about with you, *comme ça!*'

'No, no, I'm very careful really, Monsieur Poirot. As a rule it's locked up in my jewel-case, and left in the hotel safe deposit. We're staying at the Magnificent, you know. I just brought it along today for you to see.'

'And you will leave it with me, *n'est-ce pas?* You will be advised by Papa Poirot?'

'Well, you see, it's this way, Monsieur Poirot. On Friday we're going down to Yardly Chase to spend a few days with Lord and Lady Yardly.'

Her words awoke a vague echo of remembrance in my mind. Some gossip – what was it now? A few years ago Lord and Lady Yardly had paid a visit to the States, rumour had it that his lordship had rather gone the pace out there with the assistance of some lady friends – but surely there was something more, more gossip which coupled Lady Yardly's name with that of a 'movie' star in California – why! it came to me in a flash – of course it was none other than Gregory B. Rolf.

'I'll let you into a little secret, Monsieur Poirot,' Miss Marvell was continuing. 'We've got a deal on with Lord Yardly. There's some chance of our arranging to film a play down there in his ancestral pile.'

'At Yardly Chase?' I cried, interested. 'Why, it's one of the show places of England.'

Miss Marvell nodded.

'I guess it's the real old feudal stuff all right. But he wants a pretty stiff price, and of course I don't know yet whether the deal with go through, but Greg and I always like to combine business with pleasure.'

'But – I demand pardon if I am dense, madame – surely it is possible to visit Yardly Chase without taking the diamond with you?'

A shrewd, hard look came into Miss Marvell's eyes which belied their childlike appearance. She looked suddenly a good deal older.

'I want to wear it down there.'

'Surely,' I said suddenly, 'there are some very famous jewels in the Yardly collection, a large diamond amongst them.'

'That's so,' said Miss Marvell briefly.

I heard Poirot murmur beneath his breath: 'Ah, *c'est comme ça!*' Then he said aloud, with his usual uncanny luck in hitting the bull's eye (he dignifies it by the name of psychology): 'Then you are without doubt already acquainted with Lady Yardly, or perhaps your husband is?'

'Gregory knew her when she was out West three years ago,' said Miss Marvell. She hesitated a moment, and then added abruptly: 'Do either of you ever see *Society Gossip*?'

We both pleaded guilty rather shamefacedly.

'I ask because in this week's number there is an article on famous jewels, and it's really very curious – ' She broke off.

I rose, went to the table at the other side of the room and returned with the paper in question in my hand. She took it from me, found the article, and began to read aloud:

'. . . Amongst other famous stones may be included the Star of the East, a diamond in the possession of the Yardly family. An ancestor of the present Lord Yardly brought it back with him from China, and a romantic story is said to attach to it. According to this, the stone was once the right eye of a temple god. Another diamond, exactly similar in form and size, formed the left eye, and the story goes that this jewel, too, would in course of time be stolen. "One eye shall go West, the other East, till they shall meet once more. Then, in triumph shall they return to the god." It is a curious coincidence that there is at the present time a stone corresponding closely in description with this one, and known as "the Star of the West", or "the Western Star". It is the property of the celebrated film star, Miss Mary Marvell. A comparison of the two stones would be interesting.'

She stopped.

'*Epatant!*' murmured Poirot. 'Without doubt a romance of the first water.' He turned to Mary Marvell. 'And you are not afraid, madame? You have no superstitious terrors? You do not fear to introduce these two Siamese twins to each other lest a Chinaman should appear and, hey presto! whisk them both back to China?'

His tone was mocking, but I fancied that an undercurrent of seriousness lay beneath it.

'I don't believe that Lady Yardly's diamond is anything like as good as mine,' said Miss Marvell. 'Anyway, I'm going to see.'

What more Poirot would have said I do not know, for at that moment the door flew open, and a splendid-looking man strode into the room. From his crisply curling black head, to the tips of his patent-leather boots, he was a hero fit for romance.

'I said I'd call round for you, Mary,' said Gregory Rolf, 'and here I am. Well, what does Monsieur Poirot say to our little problem? Just one big hoax, same as I do?'

Poirot smiled up at the actor. They made a ridiculous contrast.

'Hoax or no hoax, Mr Rolf,' he said dryly, 'I have advised Madame your wife not to take the jewel with her to Yardly Chase on Friday.'

'I'm with you there, sir. I've already said so to Mary. But there! She's a woman through and through, and I guess she can't bear to think of another woman outshining her in the jewel line.'

'What nonsense, Gregory!' said Mary Marvell sharply. But she flushed angrily.

Poirot shrugged his shoulders.

'Madame, I have advised. I can do no more. *C'est fini.*' He bowed them both to the door.

'Ah! *la la*,' he observed, returning. '*Histoire des*

femmes! The good husband, he hit the nail on the head – *tout de même*, but he was not tactful! Assuredly not.'

I imparted to him my vague remembrances, and he nodded vigorously.

'So I thought. All the same, there is something curious underneath all this. With your permission, *mon ami*, I will take the air. Await my return, I beg of you, I shall not be long.'

I was half asleep in my chair when the landlady tapped on the door, and put her head in.

'It's another lady to see Mr Poirot, sir. I've told her he was out, but she says as how she'll wait, seeing as she's come up from the country.'

'Oh, show her in here, Mrs Murchinson. Perhaps I can do something for her.'

In another moment the lady had been ushered in. My heart gave a leap as I recognized her. Lady Yardly's portrait had figured too often in the Society papers to allow her to remain unknown.

'Do sit down, Lady Yardly,' I said, drawing forward a chair. 'My friend, Poirot is out, but I know for a fact that he'll be back very shortly.'

She thanked me and sat down. A very different type, this, from Miss Mary Marvell. Tall, dark, with flashing eyes, and a pale proud face – yet something wistful in the curves of the mouth.

I felt a desire to rise to the occasion. Why not? In Poirot's presence I have frequently felt a difficulty – I do not appear at my best. And yet there is no doubt that I, too, possess the deductive sense in a marked degree. I leant forward on a sudden impulse.

'Lady Yardly,' I said. 'I know why you have come here. You have received blackmailing letters about the diamond.'

There was no doubt as to my bolt having shot home.

She stared at me open-mouthed, all colour banished from her cheeks.

'You know?' she gasped. 'How?'

I smiled.

'By a perfectly logical process. If Miss Marvell has had warning letters – '

'Miss Marvell? She has been here?'

'She has just left. As I was saying, if she, as the holder of one of the twin diamonds, has received a mysterious series of warnings, you, as the holder of the other stone, must necessarily have done the same. You see how simple it is? I am right, then, you have received these strange communications also?'

For a moment she hesitated, as though in doubt whether to trust me or not, then she bowed her head in assent with a little smile.

'That is so,' she acknowledged.

'Were yours, too, left by hand – by a Chinaman?'

'No, they came by post; but tell me, has Miss Marvell undergone the same experience, then?'

I recounted to her the events of the morning. She listened attentively.

'It all fits in. My letters are the duplicate of hers. It is true that they came by post, but there is a curious perfume impregnating them – something in the nature of joss-stick – that at once suggested the East to me. What does it all mean?'

I shook my head.

'That is what we must find out. You have the letters with you? We might learn something from the postmarks.'

'Unfortunately I destroyed them. You understand, at the time I regarded it as some foolish joke. Can it be true that some Chinese gang are really trying to recover the diamonds? It seems too incredible.'

We went over the facts again and again, but could get

no further towards the elucidation of the mystery. At last Lady Yardly rose.

'I really don't think I need wait for Monsieur Poirot. You can tell him all this, can't you? Thank you so much Mr – '

She hesitated, her hand outstretched.

'Captain Hastings.'

'Of course! How stupid of me. You're a friend of the Cavendishes, aren't you? It was Mary Cavendish who sent me to Monsieur Poirot.'

When my friend returned, I enjoyed telling him the tale of what had occurred during his absence. He cross-questioned me rather sharply over the details of our conversation and I could read between the lines that he was not best pleased to have been absent. I also fancied that the dear old fellow was just the least inclined to be jealous. It had become rather a pose with him to consistently belittle my abilities, and I think he was chagrined at finding no loophole for criticism. I was secretly rather pleased with myself, though I tried to conceal the fact for fear of irritating him. In spite of his idiosyncrasies, I was deeply attached to my quaint little friend.

'*Bien!*' he said at length, with a curious look on his face. 'The plot develops. Pass me, I pray you, that *Peerage* on the top shelf there.' He turned the leaves. 'Ah, here we are! "Yardly . . . 10th viscount, served South African War" . . . *tout ça n'a pas d'importance* . . . "mar. 1907 Hon Maude Stopperton, fourth daughter of 3rd Baron Cotteril" . . . um, um, um . . . "has iss. two daughters, born 1908, 1910 . . . Clubs . . . residences" . . . *Voilà*, that does not tell us much. But tomorrow morning we see this *milord*!'

'What?'

'Yes. I telegraphed to him.'

'I thought you had washed your hands of the case?'

'I am not acting for Miss Marvell since she refuses to be guided by my advice. What I do now is for my own satisfaction – the satisfaction of Hercule Poirot! Decidedly, I must have a finger in this pie.'

'And you calmly wire Lord Yardly to dash up to town just to suit your convenience. He won't be pleased.'

'*Au contraire*, if I preserve for him his family diamond, he ought to be very grateful.'

'Then you really think there is a chance of it being stolen?' I asked eagerly.

'Almost a certainty,' replied Poirot placidly. 'Everything points that way.'

'But how – '

Poirot stopped my eager questions with an airy gesture of the hand.

'Not now, I pray you. Let us not confuse the mind. And observe that *Peerage* – how you have replaced him! See you not that the tallest books go in the top shelf, the next tallest in the row beneath, and so on. Thus we have order, *method*, which, as I have often told you, Hastings – '

'Exactly,' I said hastily, and put the offending volume in its proper place.

Lord Yardly turned out to be a cheery, loud-voiced sportsman with a rather red face, but with a good-humoured bonhomie about him that was distinctly attractive and made up for any lack of mentality.

'Extraordinary business this, Monsieur Poirot. Can't make head or tail of it. Seems my wife's been getting odd kind of letters, and that Miss Marvell's had 'em too. What does it all mean?'

Poirot handed him the copy of *Society Gossip*.

'First, *milord*, I would ask you if these facts are substantially correct?'

The peer took it. His face darkened with anger as he read.

'Damned nonsense!' he spluttered. 'There's never been any romantic story attaching to the diamond. It came from India originally, I believe. I never heard of all this Chinese god stuff.'

'Still, the stone *is* known as the "Star of the East".'

'Well, what if it is?' he demanded wrathfully.

Poirot smiled a little, but made no direct reply.

'What I would ask you to do, *milord*, is to place yourself in my hands. If you do so unreservedly, I have great hopes of averting the catastrophe.'

'Then you think there's actually something in these wild-cat tales?'

'Will you do as I ask you?'

'Of course I will, but – '

'*Bien!* Then permit that I ask you a few questions. This affair of Yardly Chase, is it, as you say, all fixed up between you and Mr Rolf?'

'Oh, he told you about it, did he? No, there's nothing settled.' He hesitated, the brick-red colour of his face deepening. 'Might as well get the thing straight. I've made rather an ass of myself in many ways, Monsieur Poirot – and I'm head over ears in debt – but I want to pull up. I'm fond of the kids, and I want to straighten things up, and be able to live on at the old place. Gregory Rolf is offering me big money – enough to set me on my feet again. I don't want to do it – I hate the thought of all that crowd play-acting round the Chase – but I may have to, unless – ' He broke off.

Poirot eyed him keenly. 'You have, then, another string in your bow? Permit that I make a guess? It is to sell "the Star of the East"?'

Lord Yardly nodded. 'That's it. It's been in the family for some generations, but it's not entailed. Still, it's not the easiest thing in the world to find a purchaser.

Hoffberg, the Hatton Garden man, is on the lookout for a likely customer, but he'll have to find one soon, or it's a washout.'

'One more question, *permettez* – Lady Yardly, which plan does she approve?'

'Oh, she's bitterly opposed to my selling the jewel. You know what women are. She's all for this film stunt.'

'I comprehend,' said Poirot. He remained a moment or so in thought, then rose briskly to his feet. 'You return to Yardly Chase at once? *Bien!* Say no word to anyone – to *anyone*, mind – but expect us there this evening. We will arrive shortly after five.'

'All right, but I don't see – '

'*Ça n'a pas d'importance*,' said Poirot kindly. 'You will that I preserve for you your diamond, *n'est-ce pas?*'

'Yes, but – '

'Then do as I say.'

A sadly bewildered nobleman left the room.

It was half-past five when we arrived at Yardly Chase, and followed the dignified butler to the old panelled hall with its fire of blazing logs. A pretty picture met our eyes: Lady Yardly and her two children, the mother's proud dark head bent down over the two fair ones. Lord Yardly stood near, smiling down on them.

'Monsieur Poirot and Captain Hastings,' announced the butler.

Lady Yardly looked up with a start, for her husband came forward uncertainly, his eyes seeking instruction from Poirot. The little man was equal to the occasion.

'All my excuses! It is that I investigate still this affair of Miss Marvell's. She comes to you on Friday, does she not? I make a little tour first to make sure that all is secure. Also I wanted to ask Lady Yardly if she recollected at all the postmarks on the letters she received?'

Lady Yardly shook her head regretfully. 'I'm afraid I

don't. It's stupid of me. But, you see, I never dreamt of taking them seriously.'

'You'll stay the night?' said Lord Yardly.

'Oh, *milord*, I fear to incommode you. We have left our bags at the inn.'

'That's all right.' Lord Yardly had his cue. 'We'll send down for them. No, no – no trouble, I assure you.'

Poirot permitted himself to be persuaded, and sitting down by Lady Yardly, began to make friends with the children. In a short time they were all romping together, and had dragged me into the game.

'*Vous êtes bonne mère*,' said Poirot, with a gallant little bow, as the children were removed reluctantly by a stern nurse.

Lady Yardly smoothed her ruffled hair.

'I adore them,' she said with a little catch in her voice.

'And they you – with reason!' Poirot bowed again.

A dressing-gong sounded, and we rose to go up to our rooms. At that moment the butler entered with a telegram on a salver which he handed to Lord Yardly. The latter tore it open with a brief word of apology. As he read it he stiffened visibly.

With an ejaculation he handed it to his wife. Then he glanced at my friend.

'Just a minute, Monsieur Poirot, I feel you ought to know about this. It's from Hoffberg. He thinks he's found a customer for the diamond – an American, sailing for the States tomorrow. They're sending down a chap tonight to vet the stone. By Jove, though, if this goes through – ' Words failed him.

Lady Yardly had turned away. She still held the telegram in her hand.

'I wish you wouldn't sell it, George,' she said, in a low voice. 'It's been in the family so long.' She waited, as though for a reply, but when none came her face hardened. She shrugged her shoulders. 'I must go and dress. I suppose I had better display "the goods".' She turned to Poirot with a slight grimace. 'It's one of the most hideous necklaces that was ever designed! George has always promised to have the stones reset for me, but it's never been done.' She left the room.

Half an hour later, we three were assembled in the great drawing-room awaiting the lady. It was already a few minutes past the dinner hour.

Suddenly there was a low rustle, and Lady Yardly appeared framed in the doorway, a radiant figure in a long white shimmering dress. Round the column of her neck was a rivulet of fire. She stood there with one hand just touching the necklace.

'Behold the sacrifice,' she said gaily. Her ill-humour seemed to have vanished. 'Wait while I turn the big light on and you shall feast your eyes on the ugliest necklace in England.'

The switches were just outside the door. As she stretched out her hand to them, the incredible thing happened. Suddenly without warning, every light was extinguished, the door banged, and from the other side of it came a long-drawn piercing woman's scream.

'My God!' cried Lord Yardly. 'That was Maude's voice! What has happened?'

We rushed blindly for the door, cannoning into each other in the darkness. It was some minutes before we could find it. What a sight met our eyes! Lady Yardly lay senseless on the marble floor, a crimson mark on her white throat where the necklace had been wrenched from her neck.

As we bent over her, uncertain for the moment whether she was dead or alive, her eyelids opened.

'The Chinaman,' she whispered painfully. 'The Chinaman – the side door.'

Lord Yardly sprang up with an oath. I accompanied him, my heart beating wildly. The Chinaman again! The side door in question was a small one in the angle of the wall, not more than a dozen yards from the scene of the tragedy. As we reached it, I gave a cry. There, just short of the threshold, lay the glittering necklace, evidently dropped by the thief in the panic of his flight. I swooped joyously down on it. Then I uttered another cry which Lord Yardly echoed. For in the middle of the necklace was a great gap. 'The Star of the East' was missing!

'That settles it,' I breathed. 'These were no ordinary thieves. This one stone was all they wanted.'

'But how did the fellow get in?'

'Through this door.'

'But it's always locked.'

I shook my head. 'It's not locked now. See.' I pulled it open as I spoke.

As I did so something fluttered to the ground. I picked it up. It was a piece of silk, and the embroidery was unmistakable. It had been torn from a Chinaman's robe.

'In his haste it caught in the door,' I explained. 'Come, hurry. He cannot have gone far as yet.'

But in vain we hunted and searched. In the pitch darkness of the night, the thief had found it easy to make his getaway. We returned reluctantly, and Lord Yardly sent off one of the footmen post-haste to fetch the police.

Lady Yardly, aptly ministered to by Poirot, who is as good as a woman in these matters, was sufficiently recovered to be able to tell her story.

'I was just going to turn on the other light,' she said, 'when a man sprang on me from behind. He tore my necklace from my neck with such force that I fell head-long to the floor. As I fell I saw him disappearing through the side door. Then I realized by the pig-tail and the embroidered robe that he was a Chinaman.' She stopped with a shudder.

The butler reappeared. He spoke in a low voice to Lord Yardly.

'A gentleman from Mr Hoffberg's, m'lord. He says you expect him.'

'Good heavens!' cried the distracted nobleman. 'I must see him, I suppose. No, not here, Mullings, in the library.'

I drew Poirot aside.

'Look here, my dear fellow, hadn't we better get back to London?'

'You think so, Hastings? Why?'

'Well' – I coughed delicately – 'things haven't gone very well, have they? I mean, you tell Lord Yardly to place himself in your hands and all will be well – and then the diamond vanishes from under your very nose!'

'True,' said Poirot, rather crestfallen. 'It was not one of my most striking triumphs.'

This way of describing events almost caused me to smile, but I stuck to my guns.

'So, having – pardon the expression – rather made a mess of things, don't you think it would be more graceful to leave immediately?'

'And the dinner, the without doubt excellent dinner, that the *chef* of Lord Yardly has prepared?'

'Oh, what's dinner!' I said impatiently.

Poirot held up his hands in horror.

'*Mon Dieu!* It is that in this country you treat the affairs gastronomic with a criminal indifference.'

'There's another reason why we should get back to London as soon as possible,' I continued.

'What is that my friend?'

'The other diamond,' I said, lowering my voice. 'Miss Marvell's.'

'*Eh bien*, what of it?'

'Don't you see?' His unusual obtuseness annoyed me.

What had happened to his usually keen wits? 'They've got one, now they'll go for the other.'

'*Tiens!*' cried Poirot, stepping back a pace and regarding me with admiration. 'But your brain marches to a marvel, my friend! Figure to yourself that for the moment I had not thought of that! But there is plenty of time. The full of the moon, it is not until Friday.'

I shook my head dubiously. The full of the moon theory left me entirely cold. I had my way with Poirot, however, and we departed immediately, leaving behind us a note of explanation and apology for Lord Yardly.

My idea was to go at once to the Magnificent, and relate to Miss Marvell what had occurred, but Poirot vetoed the plan, and insisted that the morning would be time enough. I gave in rather grudgingly.

In the morning Poirot seemed strangely disinclined to stir out. I began to suspect that, having made a mistake to start with, he was singularly loath to proceed with the case. In answer to my persuasions, he pointed out, with admirable common sense, that as the details of the affair at Yardly Chase were already in the morning papers the Rolfs would know quite as much as we could tell them. I gave way unwillingly.

Events proved my forebodings to be justified. About two o'clock, the telephone rang. Poirot answered it. He listened for some moments, then with a brief '*Bien, j'y serai*' he rang off, and turned to me.

'What do you think, *mon ami*?' He looked half ashamed, half excited. 'The diamond of Miss Marvell, it has been stolen.'

'What?' I cried, springing up. 'And what about the "full of the moon" now?' Poirot hung his head. 'When did this happen?'

'This morning, I understand.'

I shook my head sadly. 'If only you had listened to me. You see I was right.'

'It appears so, *mon ami*,' said Poirot cautiously. 'Appearances are deceptive, they say, but it certainly appears so.'

As we hurried in a taxi to the Magnificent, I puzzled out the true inwardness of the scheme.

'That "full of the moon" idea was clever. The whole point of it was to get us to concentrate on the Friday, and so be off our guard beforehand. It is a pity you did not realize that.'

'*Ma foi!*' said Poirot airily, his nonchalance quite restored after its brief eclipse. 'One cannot think of everything!'

I felt sorry for him. He did so hate failure of any kind.

'Cheer up,' I said consolingly. 'Better luck next time.'

At the Magnificent, we were ushered at once into the manager's office. Gregory Rolf was there with two men from Scotland Yard. A pale-faced clerk sat opposite them.

Rolf nodded to us as we entered.

'We're getting to the bottom of it,' he said. 'But it's almost unbelievable. How the guy had the nerve I can't think.'

A very few minutes sufficed to give us the facts. Mr Rolf had gone out of the hotel at 11.15. At 11.30, a gentleman, so like him in appearance as to pass muster, entered the hotel and demanded the jewel-case from the safe deposit. He duly signed the receipt, remarking carelessly as he did so: 'Looks a bit different from my ordinary one, but I hurt my hand getting out of the taxi.' The clerk merely smiled and remarked that he saw very little difference. Rolf laughed and said: 'Well, don't run me in as a crook this time, anyway. I've been getting threatening letters from a Chinaman, and the worst of it is I look rather like a Chink myself – it's something about the eyes.'

'I looked at him,' said the clerk who was telling us

this, 'and I saw at once what he meant. The eyes slanted up at the corners like an Oriental's. I'd never noticed it before.'

'Darn it all, man,' roared Gregory Rolf, leaning forward, 'do you notice it now?'

The man looked up at him and started.

'No, sir,' he said. 'I can't say I do.' And indeed there was nothing even remotely Oriental about the frank brown eyes that looked into ours.

The Scotland Yard man grunted. 'Bold customer. Thought the eyes might be noticed, and took the bull by the horns to disarm suspicion. He must have watched you out of the hotel, sir, and nipped in as soon as you were well away.'

'What about the jewel-case?' I asked. 'It was found in the corridor of the hotel. Only one thing had been taken – "the Western Star".'

We stared at each other – the whole thing was so bizarre, so unreal.

Poirot hopped briskly to his feet. 'I have not been of much use, I fear,' he said regretfully. 'Is it permitted to see Madame?'

'I guess she's prostrated with the shock,' exclaimed Rolf.

'Then perhaps I might have a few words alone with you, monsieur?'

'Certainly.'

In about five minutes Poirot reappeared.

'Now, my friend,' he said gaily. 'To a post office. I have to send a telegram.'

'Who to?'

'Lord Yardly.' He discounted further inquiries by slipping his arm through mine. 'Come, come, *mon ami*. I know all that you feel about this terrible business. I have not distinguished myself! You, in my place, might have distinguished yourself. *Bien!* All is admitted. Let us forget it and have lunch.'

It was about four o'clock when we entered Poirot's rooms. A figure rose from a chair by the window. It was Lord Yardly. He looked haggard and distraught.

'I got your wire and came up at once. Look here, I've been round to Hoffberg, and they know nothing about that man of theirs last night, or the wire either. Do you think that – '

Poirot held up his hand.

'My excuses! I sent that wire, and hired the gentleman in question.'

'*You* – but why? What?' The nobleman spluttered impotently.

'My little idea was to bring things to a head,' explained Poirot placidly.

'Bring things to a head! Oh, my God!' cried Lord Yardly.

'And the ruse succeeded,' said Poirot cheerfully. 'Therefore, *milord*, I have much pleasure in returning you – this!' With a dramatic gesture he produced a glittering object. It was a great diamond.

'The Star of the East,' gasped Lord Yardly. 'But I don't understand – '

'No?' said Poirot. 'It makes no matter. Believe me, it was necessary for the diamond to be stolen. I promised you that it would be preserved to you, and I have kept my word. You must permit me to keep my little secret. Convey, I beg of you, the assurances of my deepest respect to Lady Yardly, and tell her how pleased I am to be able to restore her jewel to her. What *beau temps*, is it not? Good Day, *milord*.'

And smiling and talking, the amazing little man conducted the bewildered nobleman to the door. He returned gently rubbing his hands.

'Poirot,' I said. 'Am I quite demented?'

'No, *mon ami*, but you are, as always, in a mental fog.'

'How did you get the diamond?'

'From Mr Rolf.'

'Rolf?'

'*Mais oui!* The warning letters, the Chinaman, the article in *Society Gossip*, all sprang from the ingenious brain of Mr Rolf! The two diamonds, supposed to be so miraculously alike – bah! they did not exist! There was only *one* diamond, my friend! Originally in the Yardly collection, for three years it has been in the possession of Mr Rolf. He stole it this morning with the assistance of a touch of grease paint at the corner of each eye! Ah, I must see him on the film, he is indeed an artist, *celui-là!*'

'But why should he steal his own diamond?' I asked, puzzled.

'For many reasons. To begin with, Lady Yardly was getting restive.'

'Lady Yardly?'

'You comprehend she was left much alone in California. Her husband was amusing himself elsewhere. Mr Rolf was handsome, he had an air about him of romance. But *au fond*, he is very business-like, *ce monsieur*! He made love to Lady Yardly, and then he blackmailed her. I taxed the lady with the truth the other night, and she admitted it. She swore that she had only been indiscreet, and I believe her. But, undoubtedly, Rolf had letters of hers that could be twisted to bear a different interpretation. Terrified by the threat of a divorce, and the prospect of being separated from her children, she agreed to all he wished. She had no money of her own, and she was forced to permit him to substitute a paste replica for the real stone. The coincidence of the date of the appearance of "the Western Star" struck me at once. All goes well. Lord Yardly prepares to range himself – to settle down. And then comes the menace of the possible sale of the diamond. The substitution will be discovered. Without doubt she writes off frantically to Gregory Rolf who has just arrived in England. He soothes her by promising to arrange all – and prepares for a double robbery. In this way he will quiet the lady, who might conceivably tell all to her husband, an affair which would not suit our blackmailer at all, he will have £50,000 insurance money (aha, you had forgotten that!), and he will still have the diamond! At this point I put my finger in the pie. The arrival of a diamond expert is announced. Lady Yardly, as I felt sure she would, immediately arranges a robbery – and does it very well too! But Hercule Poirot, he sees nothing but facts. What happens in actuality? The lady switches off the light, bangs the door, throws the necklace down the passage, and screams. She has already wrenched out the diamond with pliers upstairs – '

'But we saw the necklace round her neck!' I objected.

'I demand pardon, my friend. Her hand concealed the part of it where the gap would have shown. To place a piece of silk in the door beforehand is child's play! Of course, as soon as Rolf read of the robbery, he arranged his own little comedy. And very well he played it!'

'What did you say to him?' I asked with lively curiosity.

'I said to him that Lady Yardly had told her husband all, that I was empowered to recover the jewel, and that if it were not immediately handed over proceedings would be taken. Also a few more little lies which occurred to me. He was as wax in my hands!'

I pondered the matter.

'It seems a little unfair on Mary Marvell. She has lost her diamond through no fault of her own.'

'Bah!' said Poirot brutally. 'She has a magnificent advertisement. That is all she cares for, that one! Now the other, she is different. *Bonne mère, très femme!*'

'Yes,' I said doubtfully, hardly sharing Poirot's views on femininity. 'I suppose it was Rolf who sent her the duplicate letters.'

'*Pas du tout*,' said Poirot briskly. 'She came by the advice of Mary Cavendish to seek my aid in her dilemma. Then she heard that Mary Marvell, whom she knew to be her enemy, had been here, and she changed her mind jumping at the pretext that *you*, my friend, offered her. A very few questions sufficed to show me that *you* told her of the letters, not she you! She jumped at the chance your words offered.'

'I don't believe it,' I cried, stung.

'*Si, si, mon ami*, it is a pity you study not the psychology. She told you that the letters were destroyed? Oh, *la, la, never* does a woman destroy a letter if she can avoid it! Not even if it would be more prudent to do so!'

'It's all very well,' I said, my anger rising, 'but you've made a perfect fool of me! From beginning to end! No, it's all very well to try and explain it away afterwards. There really is a limit!'

'But you were so enjoying yourself, my friend, I had not the heart to shatter your illusions.'

'It's no good. You've gone a bit too far this time.'

'*Mon Dieu!* but how you enrage yourself for nothing, *mon ami!*'

'I'm fed up!' I went out, banging the door. Poirot had made an absolute laughing-stock of me. I decided that he needed a sharp lesson. I would let some time elapse before I forgave him. He had encouraged me to make a perfect fool of myself.

THE LOST MINE

I laid down my bank book with a sigh.

'It is a curious thing,' I observed, 'but my overdraft never seems to grow any less.'

'And it perturbs you not? Me, if I had an overdraft, never should I close my eyes all night,' declared Poirot.

'You deal in comfortable balances, I suppose!' I retorted.

'Four hundred and forty-four pounds, four and fourpence,' said Poirot with some complacency. 'A neat figure, is it not?'

'It must be tact on the part of your bank manager. He is evidently acquainted with your passion for symmetrical details. What about investing, say, three hundred of it in the Porcupine oil-fields? Their prospectus, which is advertised in the papers today, says that they will pay one hundred per cent dividends next year.'

'Not for me,' said Poirot, shaking his head. 'I like not the sensational. For me the safe, the prudent investment – *les rentes*, the consols, the – how do you call it? – the conversion.'

'Have you never made a speculative investment?'

'No, *mon ami*,' replied Poirot severely. 'I have not. And the only shares I own which have not what you call the gilded edge are fourteen thousand shares in the Burma Mines Ltd.'

Poirot paused with an air of waiting to be encouraged to go on.

'Yes?' I prompted.

'And for them I paid no cash – no, they were the

reward of the exercise of my little grey cells. You would like to hear the story? Yes?'

'Of course I would.'

'These mines are situated in the interior of Burma about two hundred miles inland from Rangoon. They were discovered by the Chinese in the fifteenth century and worked down to the time of the Mohammedan Rebellion, being finally abandoned in the year 1868. The Chinese extracted the rich lead-silver ore from the upper part of the ore body, smelting it for the silver alone, and leaving large quantities of rich lead-bearing slag. This, of course, was soon discovered when prospecting work was carried out in Burma, but owing to the fact that the old workings had become full of loose filling and water, all attempts to find the source of the ore proved fruitless. Many parties were sent out by syndicates, and they dug over a large area, but this rich prize still eluded them. But a representative of one of the syndicates got on the track of a Chinese family who were supposed to have still kept a record of the situation of the mine. The present head of the family was one Wu Ling.'

'What a fascinating page of commercial romance!' I exclaimed.

'Is it not? Ah, *mon ami*, one can have romance without golden-haired girls of matchless beauty – no, I am wrong; it is auburn hair that so excites you always. You remember – '

'Go on with the story,' I said hastily.

'*Eh bien,* my friend, this Wu Ling was approached. He was an estimable merchant, much respected in the province where he lived. He admitted at once that he owned the documents in question, and was perfectly prepared to negotiate for this sale, but he objected to dealing with anyone other than principals. Finally it was arranged that he should journey to England and meet the directors of an important company.

'Wu Ling made the journey to England in the SS *Assunta,*and the *Assunta* docked at Southampton on a cold, foggy morning in November. One of the directors, Mr Pearson, went down to Southampton to meet the boat, but owing to the fog, the train down was very much delayed, and by the time he arrived, Wu Ling had disembarked and left by special train for London. Mr Pearson returned to town somewhat annoyed, as he had no idea where the Chinaman proposed to stay. Later in the day, however, the offices of the company were rung up on the telephone. Wu Ling was staying at the Russell Square Hotel. He was feeling somewhat unwell after the voyage, but declared himself perfectly able to attend the board meeting on the following day.

'The meeting of the board took place at eleven o'clock. When half past eleven came, and Wu Ling had not put in an appearance, the secretary rang up the Russell Hotel. In answer to his inquiries, he was told that the Chinaman had gone out with a friend about half past ten. It seemed clear that he had started out with the intention of coming to the meeting, but the morning wore away, and he did not appear. It was, of course, possible that he had lost his way, being unacquainted with London, but at a late hour that night he had not returned to the hotel. Thoroughly alarmed now, Mr Pearson put matters in the hands of the police. On the following day, there was still no trace of the missing man, but towards evening of the day after that again, a body was found in the Thames which proved to be that of the ill-fated Chinaman. Neither on the body, nor in the luggage at the hotel, was there any trace of the papers relating to the mine.

'At this juncture, *mon ami,* I was brought into the affair. Mr Pearson called upon me. While profoundly shocked by the death of Wu Ling, his chief anxiety was to recover the papers which were the object of the

Chinaman's visit to England. The main anxiety of the police, of course, would be to track down the murderer – the recovery of the papers would be a secondary consideration. What he wanted me to do was to co-operate with the police while acting in the interests of the company.

'I consented readily enough. It was clear that there were two fields of search open to me. On the one hand, I might look among the employees of the company who knew of the Chinaman's coming; on the other, among the passengers on the boat who might have been acquainted with his mission. I started with the second, as being a narrower field of search. In this I coincided with Inspector Miller, who was in charge of the case – a man altogether different from our friend Japp, conceited, ill-mannered and quite insufferable. Together we interviewed the officers of the ship. They had little to ten us. Wu Ling had kept much to himself on the voyage. He had been intimate with but two of the other passengers – one a broken-down European named Dyer who appeared to bear a somewhat unsavoury reputation, the other a young bank clerk named Charles Lester, who was returning from Hong Kong. We were lucky enough to obtain snapshots of both these men. At the moment there seemed little doubt that if either of the two was implicated, Dyer was the man. He was known to be mixed up with a gang of Chinese crooks, and was altogether a most likely suspect.

'Our next step was to visit the Russell Square Hotel. Shown a snapshot of Wu Ling, they recognized him at once. We then showed them the snapshot of Dyer, but to our disappointment, the hall porter declared positively that that was not the man who had come to the hotel on the fatal morning. Almost as an afterthought, I produced the photograph of Lester, and to my surprise the man at once recognized it.

' "Yes, sir," he asserted, "that's the gentleman who came in at half past ten and asked for Mr Wu Ling, and afterwards went out with him."

'The affair was progressing. Our next move was to interview Mr Charles Lester. He met us with the utmost frankness, was desolated to hear of the Chinaman's untimely death, and put himself at our disposal in every way. His story was as follows: By arrangement with Wu Ling, he called for him at the hotel at ten-thirty. Wu Ling, however, did not appear. Instead, his servant came, explained that his master had had to go out, and offered to conduct the young man to where his master now was. Suspecting nothing, Lester agreed, and the Chinaman procured a taxi. They drove for some time in the direction of the docks. Suddenly becoming mistrustful, Lester stopped the taxi and got out, disregarding the servant's protests. That, he assured us, was all he knew.

'Apparently satisfied, we thanked him and took our leave. His story was soon proved to be a somewhat inaccurate one. To begin with, Wu Ling had had no servant with him, either on the boat or at the hotel. In the second place, the taxi driver who had driven the two men on that morning came forward. Far from Lester's having left the taxi en route, he and the Chinese gentleman had driven to a certain unsavoury dwelling-place in Limehouse, right in the heart of Chinatown. The place in question was more or less well known as an opium-den of the lowest description. The two gentlemen had gone in – about an hour later the English gentleman, whom he identified from the photograph, came out alone. He looked very pale and in, and directed the taxi-man to take him to the nearest underground station.

'Inquiries were made about Charles Lester's standing, and it was found that, though bearing an excellent character, he was heavily in debt, and had a secret passion for gambling. Dyer, of course, was not lost sight of. It seemed just faintly possible that he might have impersonated the other man, but that idea was proved utterly groundless. His alibi for the whole of the day in question was absolutely unimpeachable. Of course, the proprietor of the opium-den denied everything with Oriental stolidity. He had never seen Charles Lester. No two gentlemen had been to the place that morning. In any case, the police were wrong: no opium was ever smoked there.

'His denials, however well meant, did little to help Charles Lester. He was arrested for the murder of Wu Ling. A search of his effects was made, but no papers relating to the mine were discovered. The proprietor of the opium-den was also taken into custody, but a cursory raid of his premises yielded nothing. Not even a stick of opium rewarded the zeal of the police.

'In the meantime my friend Mr Pearson was in a great state of agitation. He strode up and down my room, uttering great lamentations.

' "But you must have some ideas, M. Poirot!" he kept urging. "Surely you must have some ideas!"

' "Certainly I have ideas," I replied cautiously. "That is the trouble – one has too many; therefore they all lead in different directions."

' "For instance?" he suggested.

' "For instance – the taxi-driver. We have only his word for it that he drove the two men to that house. That is one idea. Then – was it really that house they went to? Supposing that they left the taxi there, passed through the house and out by another entrance and went elsewhere?"

'Mr Pearson seemed struck by that.

' "But you do nothing but sit and think? Can't we *do* something?"

'He was of an impatient temperament, you comprehend.

' "Monsieur," I said with dignity, "it is not for Hercule Poirot to run up and down the evil-smelling streets of Limehouse like a little dog of no breeding. Be calm. My agents are at work."

'On the following day I had news for him. The two men had indeed passed through the house in question, but their real objective was a small eating-house close to the river. They were seen to pass in there, and Lester came out alone.

'And then, figure to yourself, Hastings, an idea of the most unreasonable seized this Mr Pearson! Nothing would suit him but that we should go ourselves to this eating-house and make investigations. I argued and prayed, but he would not listen. He talked of disguising himself – he even suggested that I – *I* should – I hesitate to say it – should shave off my moustache! Yes, *rien que ça!* I pointed out to him that that was an idea ridiculous and absurd. One destroys not a thing of beauty wantonly. Besides, shall not a Belgian gentleman with a moustache desire to see life and smoke opium just as readily as one without a moustache?

'*Eh bien,* he gave in on that, but he still insisted on his project. He turned up that evening – *Mon dieu,* what a figure! He wore what he called the "pea-jacket", his chin, it was dirty and unshaved; he had a scarf of the vilest that offended the nose. And figure to yourself, he was enjoying himself! Truly, the English are mad! He made some changes in my own appearance. I permitted it. Can one argue with a maniac? We started out – after all, could I let him go alone, a child dressed up to act the charades?'

'Of course you couldn't,' I replied.

'To continue – we arrived. Mr Pearson talked English of the strangest. He represented himself to be a man of the sea. He talked of "lubbers" and "focselles" and I know not what. It was a low little room with many Chinese in it. We ate of peculiar dishes. *Ah, Dieu, mon estomac!*' Poirot clasped that portion of his anatomy before continuing. 'Then there came to us the proprietor, a Chinaman with a face of evil smiles.

' "You gentlemen no likee food here," he said. "You come for what you likee better. Piecee pipe, eh?"

'Mr Pearson, he gave me the great kick under the table. (He had on the boots of the sea too!) And he said: "I don't mind if I do, John. Lead ahead."

'The Chinaman smiled, and he took us through a door and to a cellar and through a trapdoor, and down some steps and up again into a room all full of divans and cushions of the most comfortable. We lay down and a Chinese boy took off our boots. It was the best moment of the evening. Then they brought us the opium-pipes and cooked the opium-pills, and we pretended to smoke and then to sleep and dream. But when we were alone, Mr Pearson called softly to me, and immediately he began crawling along the floor. We went into another room where other people were asleep, and so on, until we heard two men talking. We stayed behind a curtain and listened. They were speaking of Wu Ling.

' "What about the papers?" said one.

' "Mr Lester, he takee those," answered the other, who was a Chinaman. "He say, puttee them allee in safee place – where pleeceman no lookee."

' "Ah, but he's nabbed," said the first one.

' "He gettee free. Pleeceman not sure he done it."

'There was more of the same kind of thing, then apparently the two men were coming our way, and we scuttled back to our beds.

' "We'd better get out of here," said Pearson, after a few minutes had elapsed. ' "This place isn't healthy."

' "You are right, monsieur," I agreed. "We have played the farce long enough."

'We succeeded in getting away, all right, paying handsomely for our smoke. Once clear of Limehouse, Pearson drew a long breath.

' "I'm glad to get out of that," he said. "But it's something to be sure."

' "It is indeed," I agreed. "And I fancy that we shall not have much difficulty in finding what we want – after this evening's masquerade."

'And there was no difficulty whatsoever,' finished Poirot suddenly.

This abrupt ending seemed so extraordinary that I stared at him.

'But – but where were they?' I asked.

'In his pocket – *tout simplement.*'

'But in whose pocket?'

'Mr Pearson's, *parbleu!*' Then, observing my look of bewilderment, he continued gently: 'You do not yet see it? Mr Pearson, like Charles Lester, was in debt. Mr Pearson, like Charles Lester, was fond of gambling. And he conceived the idea of stealing the papers from the Chinaman. He met him all right at Southampton, came up to London with him, and took him straight to Limehouse. It was foggy that day; the Chinaman would not notice where he was going. I fancy Mr Pearson smoked the opium fairly often down there and had some peculiar friends in consequence. I do not think he meant murder. His idea was that one of the Chinamen should impersonate Wu Ling and receive the money for the sale of the document. So far, so good! But, to the Oriental mind, it was infinitely simpler to kill Wu Ling and throw his body into the river, and Pearson's Chinese accomplices followed their own methods without consulting him. Imagine, then, what you would call the "funk *bleu*" of M. Pearson. Someone may have seen him in the train with Wu Ling – murder is a very different thing from simple abduction.

'His salvation lies with the Chinaman who is personating Wu Ling at the Russell Square Hotel. If only the body is not discovered too soon! Probably Wu Ling had told him of the arrangement between him and Charles Lester whereby the latter was to call for him at the hotel. Pearson sees there an excellent way of diverting suspicion from himself. Charles Lester shall be the last person to be seen in company with Wu Ling. The impersonator has orders to represent himself to Lester as the servant of Wu Ling, and to bring him as speedily as possible to Limehouse. There, very likely, he was offered a drink. The drink would be suitably drugged, and when Lester emerged an hour later, he would have a very hazy impression of what had happened. So much was this the case, that as soon as Lester learned of Wu Ling's death, he loses his nerve, and denies that he ever reached Limehouse.

'By that, of course, he plays right into Pearson's hands. But is Pearson content? No – my manner disquiets him, and he determines to complete the case against Lester. So he arranges an elaborate masquerade. Me, I am to be gulled completely. Did I not say just now that he was as a child acting the charades? *Eh bien*, I play my part. He goes home rejoicing. But in the morning, Inspector Miller arrives on his doorstep. The papers are found on him; the game is up. Bitterly he regrets permitting himself to play the farce with Hercule Poirot! There was only one real difficulty in the affair.'

'What was that?' I demanded curiously.

'Convincing Inspector Miller! What an animal, that! Both obstinate and imbecile. And in the end he took half the credit!'

'Too bad,' I cried.

'Ah, well, I had my compensations. The other

directors of the Burma Mines Ltd awarded me fourteen thousand shares as a small recompense for my services. Not so bad, eh? But when investing money, keep, I beg of you, Hastings, strictly to the conservative. The things you read in the paper, they may not be true. The directors of the Porcupine – they may be so many Mr Pearsons!'

THE KIDNAPPED PRIME MINISTER

Now that war and the problems of war are things of the past, I think I may safely venture to reveal to the world the part which my friend Poirot played in a moment of national crisis. The secret has been well guarded. Not a whisper of it reached the Press. But, now that the need for secrecy has gone by, I feel it is only just that England should know the debt it owes to my quaint little friend, whose marvellous brain so ably averted a great catastrophe.

One evening after dinner – I will not particularize the date; it suffices to say that it was at the time when 'Peace by negotiation' was the parrot-cry of England's enemies – my friend and I were sitting in his rooms. After being invalided out of the Army I had been given a recruiting job, and it had become my custom to drop in on Poirot in the evenings after dinner and talk with him of any cases of interest that he might have had on hand.

I was attempting to discuss with him the sensational news of the day – no less than an attempted assassination of Mr David MacAdam, England's Prime Minister. The account in the papers had evidently been carefully censored. No details were given, save that the Prime Minister had had a marvellous escape, the bullet just grazing his cheek.

I considered that our police must have been shamefully careless for such an outrage to be possible. I could well understand that the German agents in England would be willing to risk much for such an achievement. 'Fighting Mac', as his own party had nicknamed him, had strenuously and unequivocally combated the Pacifist influence which was becoming so prevalent.

He was more than England's Prime Minister – he *was* England; and to have removed him from his sphere of influence would have been a crushing and paralysing blow to Britain.

Poirot was busy mopping a grey suit with a minute sponge. Never was there a dandy such as Hercule Poirot. Neatness and order were his passion. Now, with the odour of benzene filling the air, he was quite unable to give me his full attention.

'In a little minute I am with you, my friend. I have all but finished. The spot of grease – he is not good – I remove him – so!' He waved his sponge.

I smiled as I lit another cigarette.

'Anything interesting on?' I inquired, after a minute or two.

'I assist a – how do you call it? – "charlady" to find her husband. A difficult affair, needing the tact. For I have a little idea that when he is found he will not be pleased. What would you? For my part, I sympathize with him. He was a man of discrimination to lose himself.'

I laughed.

'At last! The spot of grease, he is gone! I am at your disposal.'

'I was asking you what you thought of this attempt to assassinate MacAdam?'

'*Enfantillage!*' replied Poirot promptly. 'One can hardly take it seriously. To fire with the rifle – never does it succeed. It is a device of the past.'

'It was very near succeeding this time,' I reminded him.

Poirot shook his head impatiently. He was about to reply when the landlady thrust her head round the door and informed him that there were two gentlemen below who wanted to see him.

'They won't give their names, sir, but they says as it's very important.'

'Let them mount,' said Poirot, carefully folding his grey trousers.

In a few minutes the two visitors were ushered in, and my heart gave a leap as in the foremost I recognized no less a personage than Lord Estair, Leader of the House of Commons; whilst his companion, Mr Bernard Dodge, was also a member of the War Cabinet, and, as I knew, a close personal friend of the Prime Minister.

'Monsieur Poirot?' said Lord Estair interrogatively. My friend bowed. The great man looked at me and hesitated. 'My business is private.'

'You may speak freely before Captain Hastings,' said my friend, nodding to me to remain. 'He has not all the gifts, no! But I answer for his discretion.'

Lord Estair still hesitated, but Mr Dodge broke in abruptly:

'Oh, come on – don't let's beat about the bush! As far as I can see, the whole of England will know the hole we're in soon enough. Time's everything.'

'Pray be seated, messieurs,' said Poirot politely. 'Will you take the big chair, *milord*?'

Lord Estair started slightly. 'You know me?'

Poirot smiled. 'Certainly. I read the little papers with the pictures. How should I not know you?'

'Monsieur Poirot, I have come to consult you upon a matter of the most vital urgency. I must ask for absolute secrecy.'

'You have the word of Hercule Poirot – I can say no more' said my friend grandiloquently.

'It concerns the Prime Minister. We are in grave trouble.'

'We're up a tree!' interposed Mr Dodge.

'The injury is serious then?' I asked.

'What injury?'

'The bullet wound.'

'Oh, that!' cried Mr Dodge contemptuously. 'That's old history.'

'As my colleague says,' continued Lord Estair, 'that affair is over and done with. Luckily, it failed. I wish I could say as much for the second attempt.'

'There has been a second attempt, then?'

'Yes, though not of the same nature. Monsieur Poirot, the Prime Minister has disappeared.'

'What?'

'He has been kidnapped!'

'Impossible!' I cried, stupefied.

Poirot threw a withering glance at me, which I knew enjoined me to keep my mouth shut.

'Unfortunately, impossible as it seems, it is only too true,' continued his lordship.

Poirot looked at Mr Dodge. 'You said just now, monsieur, that time was everything. What did you mean by that?'

The two men exchanged glances, and then Lord Estair said:

'You have heard, Monsieur Poirot, of the approaching Allied Conference?'

My friend nodded.

'For obvious reasons, no details have been given of when and where it is to take place. But, although it has been kept out of the newspapers, the date is, of course, widely known in diplomatic circles. The Conference is to be held tomorrow – Thursday – evening at Versailles. Now you perceive the terrible gravity of the situation. I will not conceal from you that the Prime Minister's presence at the Conference is a vital necessity. The Pacifist propaganda, started and maintained by the German agents in our midst, has been very active. It is the universal opinion that the turning-point of the Conference will be the strong personality of the Prime Mini-

ster. His absence may have the most serious results –
possibly a premature and disastrous peace. And we
have no one who can be sent in his place. He alone
can represent England.'

Poirot's face had grown very grave. 'Then you regard
the kidnapping of the Prime Minister as a direct attempt
to prevent his being present at the Conference?'

'Most certainly I do. He was actually on his way to
France at the time.'

'And the Conference is to be held?'

'At nine o'clock tomorrow night.'

Poirot drew an enormous watch from his pocket.

'It is now a quarter to nine.'

'Twenty-four hours,' said Mr Dodge thoughtfully.

'And a quarter,' amended Poirot. 'Do not forget the
quarter, monsieur – it may come in useful. Now for the
details – the abduction, did it take place in England or
in France?'

'In France. Mr MacAdam crossed to France this
morning. He was to stay to-night as the guest of the
Commander-in-Chief, proceeding tomorrow to Paris. He
was conveyed across the Channel by destroyer. At Boulogne he was met by a car from General Headquarters
and one of the Commander-in-Chief's ADCs.'

'*Eh bien?*'

'Well, they started from Boulogne – but they never
arrived.'

'What?'

'Monsieur Poirot, it was a bogus car and a bogus
ADC. The real car was found in a side road, with the
chauffeur and the ADC neatly gagged and bound.'

'And the bogus car?'

'Is still at large.'

Poirot made a gesture of impatience. 'Incredible!
Surely it cannot escape attention for long?'

'So we thought. It seemed merely a question of searching thoroughly. That part of France is under Military Law. We were convinced that the car could not go long unnoticed. The French police and our own Scotland Yard men, and the military are straining every nerve. It is, as you say, incredible – but nothing has been discovered!'

At that moment a tap came at the door, and a young officer entered with a heavily sealed envelope which he handed to Lord Estair.

'Just through from France, sir. I brought it on here, as you directed.'

The Minister tore it open eagerly, and uttered an exclamation. The officer withdrew.

'Here is news at last! This telegram has just been decoded. They have found the second car, also the secretary, Daniels, chloroformed, gagged, and bound, in an abandoned farm near C – . He remembers nothing, except something being pressed against his mouth and nose from behind, and struggling to free himself. The police are satisfied as to the genuineness of his statement.'

'And they have found nothing else?'

'No.'

'Not the Prime Minister's dead body? Then, there is hope. But it is strange. Why, after trying to shoot him this morning, are they now taking so much trouble to keep him alive?'

Dodge shook his head. 'One thing's quite certain. They're determined at all costs to prevent his attending the Conference.'

'If it is humanly possible, the Prime Minister shall be there. God grant it is not too late. Now, messieurs, recount to me everything – from the beginning. I must know about this shooting affair as well.'

'Last night, the Prime Minister, accompanied by one of his secretaries, Captain Daniels – '

'The same who accompanied him to France?'

'Yes. As I was saying, they motored down to Windsor, where the Prime Minister was granted an Audience. Early this morning he returned to town, and it was on the way that the attempted assassination took place.'

'One moment, if you please. Who is this Captain Daniels? You have his dossier?'

Lord Estair smiled. 'I thought you would ask me that. We do not know very much of him. He is of no particular family. He has served in the English Army, and is an extremely able secretary, being an exceptionally fine linguist. I believe he speaks seven languages. It is for that reason that the Prime Minister chose him to accompany him to France.'

'Has he any relatives in England?'

'Two Aunts. A Mrs Everard, who lives at Hampstead, and a Miss Daniels, who lives near Ascot.'

'Ascot? That is near to Windsor, is it not?'

'That point has not been overlooked. But it has led to nothing.'

'You regard the Capitaine Daniels, then, as above suspicion?'

A shade of bitterness crept into Lord Estair's voice, as he replied:

'No, Monsieur Poirot. In these days, I should hesitate before I pronounced *anyone* above suspicion.'

'*Très bien.* Now I understand, *milord*, that the Prime Minister would, as a matter of course, be under vigilant police protection, which ought to render any assault upon him an impossibility?'

Lord Estair bowed his head. 'That is so. The Prime Minister's car was closely followed by another car containing detectives in plain clothes. Mr MacAdam knew nothing of these precautions. He is personally a most fearless man, and would be inclined to sweep them away arbitrarily. But, naturally, the police make their own arrangements. In fact, the Premier's chauffeur, O'Murphy, is a CID man.'

'O'Murphy? That is a name of Ireland, is it not so?'

'Yes, he is an Irishman.'

'From what part of Ireland?'

'County Clare, I believe.'

'*Tiens!* But proceed, *milord.*'

'The Premier started for London. The car was a closed one. He and Captain Daniels sat inside. The second car followed as usual. But, unluckily, for some unknown reason, the Prime Minister's car deviated from the main road – '

'At a point where the road curves?' interrupted Poirot.

'Yes – but how did you know?'

'Oh, *c'est evident!* Continue!'

'For some unknown reason,' continued Lord Estair, 'the Premier's car left the main road. The police car, unaware of the deviation, continued to keep to the high road. At a short distance down the unfrequented lane, the Prime Minister's car was suddenly held up by a band of masked men. The chauffeur – '

'That brave O'Murphy' murmured Poirot thoughtfully.

'The chauffeur, momentarily taken aback, jammed on the brakes. The Prime Minister put his head out of the window. Instantly a shot rang out – then another. The first one grazed his cheek, the second, fortunately, went wide. The chauffeur, now realizing the danger, instantly forged straight ahead, scattering the band of men.'

'A near escape,' I ejaculated, with a shiver.

'Mr MacAdam refused to make any fuss over the slight wound he had received. He declared it was only a scratch. He stopped at a local cottage hospital, where it was dressed and bound up – he did not, of course, reveal his identity. He then drove, as per schedule, straight to Charing Cross, where a special train for Dover was awaiting him, and, after a brief account of what had happened had been given to the anxious police by Captain Daniels, he duly departed for France. At Dover, he went on board the waiting destroyer. At Boulogne, as you know, the bogus car was waiting for him, carrying the Union jack, and correct in every detail.'

'That is all you have to tell me?'

'Yes.'

'There is no other circumstance that you have omitted, *milord*?'

'Well, there is one rather peculiar thing.'

'Yes?'

'The Prime Minister's car did not return home after leaving the Prime Minister at Charing Cross. The police were anxious to interview O'Murphy, so a search was instituted at once. The car was discovered standing outside a certain unsavoury little restaurant in Soho, which is well known as a meeting-place of German agents.'

'And the chauffeur?'

'The chauffeur was nowhere to be found. He, too, had disappeared.'

'So,' said Poirot thoughtfully, 'there are two disappearances: the Prime Minister in France, and O'Murphy in London.'

He looked keenly at Lord Estair, who made a gesture of despair.

'I can only tell you, Monsieur Poirot, that, if anyone had suggested to me yesterday that O'Murphy was a traitor, I should have laughed in his face.'

'And today?'

'Today I do not know what to think.'

Poirot nodded gravely. He looked at his turnip of a watch again.

'I understand that I have *carte blanche*, messieurs – in every way, I mean? I must be able to go where I choose, and how I choose.'

'Perfectly. There is a special train leaving for Dover in an hour's time, with a further contingent from Scotland Yard. You shall be accompanied by a Military officer and a CID man, who will hold themselves at your disposal in every way. Is that satisfactory?'

'Quite. One more question before you leave, messieurs. What made you come to me? I am unknown, obscure in this great London of yours.'

'We sought you out on the express recommendation and wish of a very great man of your own country.'

'*Comment*? My old friend the *Préfet* – ?'

Lord Estair shook his head.

'One higher than the *Préfet*. One whose word was once law in Belgium – and shall be again! That England has sworn!'

Poirot's hand flew swiftly to a dramatic salute. 'Amen to that! Ah, but my Master does not forget . . . Messieurs, I, Hercule Poirot, will serve you faithfully. Heaven only send that it will be in time. But this is dark – dark . . . I cannot see.'

'Well, Poirot,' I cried impatiently, as the door closed behind the Ministers, 'what do you think?'

My friend was busy packing a minute suitcase, with quick, deft movements. He shook his head thoughtfully.

'I don't know what to think. My brains desert me.'

'Why, as you said, kidnap him, when a knock on the head would do as well?' I mused.

'Pardon me, *mon ami*, but I did not quite say that. It is undoubtedly far more their affair to kidnap him.'

'But why?'

'Because uncertainty creates panic. That is one reason. Were the Prime Minister dead, it would be a terrible calamity, but the situation would have to be faced. But now you have paralysis. Will the Prime Minister reappear, or will he not? Is he dead or alive? Nobody knows, and until they know nothing definite can be done: And, as I tell you, uncertainty breeds panic, which is what *les Bosches* are playing for. Then, again, if the kidnappers are holding him secretly somewhere, they have the advantage of being able to make terms with both sides. The German Government is not a liberal paymaster, as a rule, but no doubt they can be made to disgorge substantial remittances in such a case as this. Thirdly, they run no risk of the hangman's rope. Oh, decidedly, kidnapping is their affair.'

'Then, if that is so, why should they first try to shoot him?'

Poirot made a gesture of anger. 'Ah, that is just what I do not understand! It is inexplicable – stupid! They have all their arrangements made (and very good arrangements too) for the abduction, and yet they imperil the whole affair by a melodramatic attack, worthy of a cinema, and quite as unreal. It is almost impossible to believe in it, with its band of masked men, not twenty miles from London!'

'Perhaps they were two quite separate attempts which happened irrespective of each other,' I suggested.

'Ah, no, that would be too much of a coincidence! Then, further – who is the traitor? There must have been a traitor – in the first affair, anyway. But who was it – Daniels or O'Murphy? It must have been one of the two, or why did the car leave the main road? We cannot suppose that the Prime Minister connived at his own assassination! Did O'Murphy take that turning of his own accord, or was it Daniels who told him to do so?'

'Surely it must have been O'Murphy's doing.'

'Yes, because if it was Daniels' the Prime Minister would have heard the order, and would have asked the reason. But there are altogether too many "whys" in this affair, and they contradict each other. If O'Murphy is an honest man, *why* did he leave the main road? But if he was a dishonest man, *why* did he start the car again when only two shots had been fired – thereby, in all probability, saving the Prime Minister's life? And, again, if he was honest, why did he, immediately on leaving Charing Cross, drive to a well-known rendezvous of German spies?'

'It looks bad,' I said.

'Let us look at the case with method. What have we for and against these two men? Take O'Murphy first. Against: that his conduct in leaving the main road was suspicious; that he is an Irishman from County Clare; that he has disappeared in a highly suggestive manner. For: that his promptness in restarting the car saved the Premier's life; that he is a Scotland Yard man, and, obviously, from the post allotted to him, a trusted detective. Now for Daniels. There is not much against him, except the fact that nothing is known of his antecedents, and that he speaks too many languages for a good Englishman! (Pardon me, *mon ami*, but, as linguists, you are deplorable!) Now *for* him, we have the fact that he was found gagged, bound, and chloroformed – which does not look as though he had anything to do with the matter.'

'He might have gagged and bound himself, to divert suspicion.'

Poirot shook his head. 'The French police would make no mistake of that kind. Besides, once he had attained his object, and the Prime Minister was safely abducted, there would not be much point in his remaining behind. His accomplices *could* have gagged and chloroformed him, of course, but I fail to see what object they hoped to accomplish by it. He can be of little use to them now, for, until the circumstances concerning the Prime Minister have been cleared up, he is bound to be closely watched.'

'Perhaps he hoped to start the police on a false scent?'

'Then why did he not do so? He merely says that

something was pressed over his nose and mouth, and that he remembers nothing more. There is no false scent there. It sounds remarkably like the truth.'

'Well,' I said, glancing at the clock, 'I suppose we'd better start for the station. You may find more clues in France.'

'Possibly, *mon ami*, but I doubt it. It is still incredible to me that the Prime Minister has not been discovered in that limited area, where the difficulty of concealing him must be tremendous. If the military and the police of two countries have not found him, how shall I?'

At Charing Cross we were met by Mr Dodge.

'This is Detective Barnes, of Scotland Yard, and Major Norman. They will hold themselves entirely at your disposal. Good luck to you. It's a bad business, but I've not given up hope. Must be off now.' And the Minister strode rapidly away.

We chatted in a desultory fashion with Major Norman. In the centre of the little group of men on the platform I recognized a little ferret-faced fellow talking to a tall, fair man. He was an old acquaintance of Poirot's – Detective-Inspector Japp, supposed to be one of the smartest of Scotland Yard's officers. He came over and greeted my friend cheerfully.

'I heard you were on this job too. Smart bit of work. So far they've got away with the goods all right. But I can't believe they can keep him hidden long. Our people are going through France with a toothcomb. So are the French. I can't help feeling it's only a matter of hours now.

'That is, if he's still alive,' remarked the tall detective gloomily.

Japp's face fell. 'Yes . . . but somehow I've got the feeling he's still alive all right.'

Poirot nodded. 'Yes, yes; he's alive. But can he be

found in time? I, like you, did not believe he could be hidden so long.'

The whistle blew, and we all trooped up into the Pullman car. Then, with a slow, unwilling jerk, the train drew out of the station.

It was a curious journey. The Scotland Yard men crowded together. Maps of Northern France were spread out, and eager forefingers traced the lines of roads and villages. Each man had his own pet theory. Poirot showed none of his usual loquacity, but sat staring in front of him, with an expression on his face that reminded me of a puzzled child. I talked to Norman, whom I found quite an amusing fellow. On arriving at Dover Poirot's behaviour moved me to intense amusement. The little man, as he went on board the boat, clutched desperately at my arm. The wind was blowing lustily.

'*Mon Dieu*' he murmured. 'This is terrible!'

'Have courage, Poirot,' I cried. 'You will succeed. You will find him. I am sure of it.'

'Ah, *mon ami*, you mistake my emotion. It is this villainous sea that troubles me! The *mal de mer* – it is horrible suffering!'

'Oh!' I said, rather taken aback.

The first throb of the engines was felt, and Poirot groaned and closed his eyes.

'Major Norman has a map of Northern France if you would like to study it?'

Poirot shook his head impatiently.

'But no, but no! Leave me, my friend. See you, to think, the stomach and the brain must be in harmony. Laverguier has a method most excellent for averting the *mal de mer*. You breathe in – and out – slowly, so – turning the head from left to right and counting six between each breath.'

I left him to his gymnastic endeavours, and went on deck.

As we came slowly into Boulogne Harbour Poirot appeared, neat and smiling, and announced to me in a whisper that Laverguier's system had succeeded 'to a marvel!'

Japp's forefinger was still tracing imaginary routes on his map. 'Nonsense! The car started from Boulogne – here they branched off. Now, my idea is that they transferred the Prime Minister to another car. See?'

'Well,' said the tall detective, 'I shall make for the seaports. Ten to one, they've smuggled him on board a ship.'

Japp shook his head. 'Too obvious. The order went out at once to close all the ports.'

The day was just breaking as we landed. Major Norman touched Poirot on the arm. 'There's a military car here waiting for you, sir.'

'Thank you, monsieur. But, for the moment, I do not propose to leave Boulogne.'

'What?'

'No, we will enter this hotel here, by the quay.'

He suited the action to the word, demanded and was accorded a private room. We three followed him, puzzled and uncomprehending.

He shot a quick glance at us. 'It is not so that the good detective should act, eh? I perceive your thought. He must be full of energy. He must rush to and fro. He should prostrate himself on the dusty road and seek the marks of tyres through a little glass. He must gather up the cigarette-end, the fallen match? That is your idea, is it not?'

His eyes challenged us. 'But I – Hercule Poirot – tell you that it is not so! The true clues are within – *here*!' He tapped his forehead. 'See you, I need not have left London. It would have been sufficient for me to sit quietly in my rooms there. All that matters is the little grey cells within. Secretly and silently they do their part, until suddenly I call for a map, and I lay my finger on a spot – so – and I say: the Prime Minister is *there*! And it is so! With method and logic one can accomplish anything! This frantic rushing to France was a mistake – it is playing a child's game of hide-and-seek. But now, though it may be too late, I will set to work the right way, from within. Silence, my friends, I beg of you.'

And for five long hours the little man sat motionless, blinking his eyelids like a cat, his green eyes flickering and becoming steadily greener and greener. The Scotland Yard man was obviously contemptuous, Major Norman was bored and impatient, and I myself found the time pass with wearisome slowness.

Finally, I got up, and strolled as noiselessly as I could to the window. The matter was becoming a farce. I was secretly concerned for my friend. If he failed, I would have preferred him to fail in a less ridiculous manner. Out of the window I idly watched the daily leave boat, belching forth columns of smoke, as she lay alongside the quay.

Suddenly I was aroused by Poirot's voice close to my elbow.

'*Mes amis*, let us start!'

I turned. An extraordinary transformation had come over my friend. His eyes were flickering with excitement, his chest was swelled to the uttermost.

'I have been an imbecile, my friends! But I see daylight at last.'

Major Norman moved hastily to the door. 'I'll order the car.'

'There is no need. I shall not use it. Thank Heaven the wind has fallen.'

'Do you mean you are going to walk, sir?'

'No, my young friend. I am no St Peter. I prefer to cross the sea by boat.'

'To cross the *sea*?'

'Yes. To work with method, one must begin from the beginning. And the beginning of this affair was in England. Therefore, we return to England.'

At three o'clock, we stood once more upon Charing Cross platform. To all our expostulations, Poirot turned a deaf ear, and reiterated again and again that to start at the beginning was not a waste of time, but the only way. On the way over, he had conferred with Norman in a low voice, and the latter had despatched a sheaf of telegrams from Dover.

Owing to the special passes held by Norman, we got through everywhere in record time. In London, a large police car was waiting for us, with some plain-clothes men, one of whom handed a typewritten sheet of paper to my friend. He answered my inquiring glance.

'A list of the cottage hospitals within a certain radius west of London. I wired for it from Dover.'

We were whirled rapidly through the London streets. We were on the Bath Road. On we went, through Hammersmith, Chiswick and Brentford. I began to see our objective. Through Windsor and so on to Ascot. My heart gave a leap. Ascot was where Daniels had an aunt living. We were after him, then, not O'Murphy.

We duly stopped at the gate of a trim villa. Poirot jumped out and rang the bell. I saw a perplexed frown dimming the radiance of his face. Plainly, he was not satisfied. The bell was answered. He was ushered inside. In a few moments he reappeared, and climbed into the car with a short, sharp shake of his head. My hopes began to die down. It was past four now. Even if he found certain evidence incriminating Daniels, what would be the good of it, unless he could wring from someone the exact spot in France where they were holding the Prime Minister?

Our return progress towards London was an interrupted one. We deviated from the main road more than once, and occasionally stopped at a small building, which I had no difficulty in recognizing as a cottage hospital. Poirot only spent a few minutes at each, but at every halt his radiant assurance was more and more restored.

He whispered something to Norman, to which the latter replied:

'Yes, if you turn off to the left, you will find them waiting by the bridge.'

We turned up a side road, and in the failing light I discerned a second car, waiting by the side of the road. It contained two men in plain clothes. Poirot got down and spoke to them, and then we started off in a northerly direction, the other car following close behind.

We drove for some time, our objective being obviously one of the northern suburbs of London. Finally, we drove up to the front door of a tall house, standing a little back from the road in its own grounds.

Norman and I were left with the car. Poirot and one of the detectives went up to the door and rang. A neat parlourmaid opened it. The detective spoke.

'I am a police officer, and I have a warrant to search this house.'

The girl gave a little scream, and a tall, handsome woman of middle-age appeared behind her in the hall.

'Shut the door, Edith. They are burglars, I expect.'

But Poirot swiftly inserted his foot in the door, and at the same moment blew a whistle. Instantly the other detectives ran up, and poured into the house, shutting the door behind them.

Norman and I spent about five minutes cursing our forced inactivity. Finally the door reopened, and the men emerged, escorting three prisoners – a woman and two men. The woman, and one of the men, were taken to the second car. The other man was placed in our car by Poirot himself.

'I must go with the others, my friend. But have great care of this gentleman. You do not know him, no? *Eh bien*, let me present to you, Monsieur O'Murphy!'

O'Murphy! I *gaped* at him open-mouthed as we started again. He was not handcuffed, but I did not fancy he would try to escape. He sat there staring in front of him as though dazed. Anyway, Norman and I would be more than a match for him.

To my surprise, we still kept a northerly route. We were not returning to London, then! I was much puzzled. Suddenly, as the car slowed down, I recognized that we were close to Hendon Aerodrome. Immediately I grasped Poirot's idea. He proposed to reach France by aeroplane.

It was a sporting idea, but, on the face of it, impracticable. A telegram would be far quicker. Time was everything. He must leave the personal glory of rescuing the Prime Minister to others.

As we drew up, Major Norman jumped out, and a plain-clothes man took his place. He conferred with Poirot for a few minutes, and then went off briskly.

I, too, jumped out, and caught Poirot by the arm.

'I congratulate you, old fellow They have told you the hiding-place? But, look here, you must wire to France at once. You'll be too late if you go yourself.'

Poirot looked at me curiously for a minute or two.

'Unfortunately, my friend, there are some things that cannot be sent by telegram.'

At that moment Major Norman returned, accompanied by a young officer in the uniform of the Flying Corps.

'This is Captain Lyall, who will fly you over to France. He can start at once.'

'Wrap up warmly, sir,' said the young pilot. 'I can lend you a coat, if you like.'

Poirot was consulting his enormous watch. He murmured to himself: 'Yes, there is time – just time.' Then he looked up and bowed politely to the young officer. 'I thank you, monsieur. But it is not I who am your passenger. It is this gentleman here.'

He moved a little aside as he spoke, and a figure came forward out of the darkness. It was the second male prisoner who had gone in the other car, and as the light fell on his face, I gave a start of surprise.

It was the Prime Minister!

'For Heaven's sake, tell me all about it,' I cried impatiently, as Poirot, Norman and I motored back to London. 'How in the world did they manage to smuggle him back to England?'

'There was no need to smuggle him back,' replied Poirot dryly. 'The Prime Minister has never left England. He was kidnapped on his way from Windsor to London.'

'*What?*'

'I will make all clear. The Prime Minister was in his car, his secretary beside him. Suddenly a pad of chloroform is clapped on his face – '

'But by whom?'

'By the clever linguistic Captain Daniels. As soon as the Prime Minister is unconscious, Daniels picks up the speaking-tube, and directs O'Murphy to turn to the right, which the chauffeur, quite unsuspicious, does. A few yards down that unfrequented road a large car is standing, apparently broken down. Its driver signals to O'Murphy to stop. O'Murphy slows up. The stranger approaches. Daniels leans out of the window, and, probably with the aid of an instantaneous anaesthetic, such as ethylchloride, the chloroform trick is repeated. In a few seconds, the two helpless men are dragged out and transferred to the other car, and a pair of substitutes take their places.'

'Impossible'

'*Pas du tout*! Have you not seen music-hall turns imitating celebrities with marvellous accuracy? Nothing is easier than to personate a pubic character. The Prime Minister of England is far easier to understudy than Mr John Smith of Clapham, say. As for O'Murphy's "double", no one was going to take much notice of him until after the departure of the Prime Minister, and by then he would have made himself scarce. He drives straight from Charing Cross to the meeting-place of his friends. He goes in as O'Murphy, he emerges as someone quite different. O'Murphy has disappeared, leaving a conveniently suspicious trail behind him.'

'But the man who personated the Prime Minister was seen by everyone!'

'He was not seen by anyone who knew him privately or intimately. And Daniels shielded him from contact with anyone as much as possible. Moreover, his face was bandaged up, and anything unusual in his manner would be put down to the fact that he was suffering from shock as a result of the attempt upon his life. Mr MacAdam has a weak throat, and always spares his voice as much as possible before any great speech. The deception was perfectly easy to keep up as far as France. There it would be impracticable and impossible – so the Prime Minister disappears. The police of this country hurry across the Channel, and no one bothers to go into the details of the first attack. To sustain the illusion that the abduction has taken place in France, Daniels is gagged and chloroformed in a convincing manner.'

'And the man who has enacted the part of the Prime Minister?'

'Rids himself of his disguise. He and the bogus chauffeur may be arrested as suspicious characters, but no one will dream of suspecting their real part in the drama, and they will eventually be released for lack of evidence.'

'And the real Prime Minister?'

'He and O'Murphy were driven straight to the house of "Mrs Everard," at Hampstead, Daniels' so-called "aunt". In reality, she is Frau Bertha Ebenthal, and the police have been looking for her for some time. It is a valuable little present that I have made them – to say nothing of Daniels! Ah, it was a clever plan, but he did not reckon on the cleverness of Hercule Poirot!'

I think my friend might well be excused his moment of vanity.

'When did you first begin to suspect the truth of the matter?'

'When I began to work the right way – from *within*! I could not make that shooting affair fit in – but when I saw that the net result of it was that *the Prime Minister went to France with his face bound up* I began to comprehend! And when I visited all the cottage hospitals between Windsor and London, and found that no one answering to my description had had his face bound up and dressed that morning, I was sure! After that, it was child's play for a mind like mine!'

The following morning, Poirot showed me a telegram he had just received. It had no place of origin, and was unsigned. It ran:

'In time.'

Later in the day the evening papers published an account of the Allied Conference. They laid particular stress on the magnificent ovation accorded to Mr David MacAdam, whose inspiring speech had produced a deep and lasting impression.

THE DISAPPEARANCE OF MR DAVENHEIM

Poirot and I were expecting our old friend Inspector Japp of Scotland Yard to tea. We were sitting round the tea-table awaiting his arrival. Poirot had just finished carefully straightening the cups and saucers which our landlady was in the habit of throwing, rather than placing, on the table. He had also breathed heavily on the metal teapot, and polished it with a silk handkerchief. The kettle was on the boil, and a small enamel saucepan beside it contained some thick, sweet chocolate which was more to Poirot's palate than what he described as 'your English poison'.

A sharp 'rat-tat' sounded below, and a few minutes afterwards Japp entered briskly.

'Hope I'm not late,' he said as he greeted us. 'To tell the truth, I was yarning with Miller, the man who's in charge of the Davenheim case.'

I pricked up my ears. For the last three days the papers had been full of the strange disappearance of Mr Davenheim, senior partner of Davenheim and Salmon, the well-known bankers and financiers. On Saturday last he had walked out of his house, and had never been seen since. I looked forward to extracting some interesting details from Japp.

'I should have thought,' I remarked, 'that it would be almost impossible for anyone to "disappear" nowadays.'

Poirot moved a plate of bread and butter the eighth of an inch, and said sharply:

'Be exact, my friend. What do you mean by "disappear"? To which class of disappearance are you referring?'

'Are disappearances classified and labelled, then?' I laughed.

Japp smiled also. Poirot frowned at both of us.

'But certainly they are! They fall into three categories: First, and most common, the voluntary disappearance. Second, the much abused "loss of memory" case – rare, but occasionally genuine. Third, murder, and a more or less successful disposal of the body. Do you refer to all three as impossible of execution?'

'Very nearly so, I should think. You might lose your own memory, but someone would be sure to recognize you – especially in the case of a well-known man like Davenheim. Then "bodies" can't be made to vanish into thin air. Sooner or later they turn up, concealed in lonely places, or in trunks. Murder will out. In the same way, the absconding clerk, or the domestic defaulter, is bound to be run down in these days of wireless telegraphy. He can be headed off from foreign countries; ports and railway stations are watched; and as for concealment in this country, his features and appearance will be known to everyone who reads a daily newspaper. He's up against civilization.'

'*Mon ami,*' said Poirot, 'you make one error. You do not allow for the fact that a man who had decided to make away with another man – or with himself in a figurative sense – might be that rare machine, a man of method. He might bring intelligence, talent, a careful calculation of detail to the task; and then I do not see why he should not be successful in baffling the police force.'

But not *you*, I suppose?' said Japp good-humouredly, winking at me. 'He couldn't baffle you, eh, Monsieur Poirot?'

Poirot endeavoured, with a marked lack of success, to

look modest. 'Me also! Why not? It is true that I approach such problems with an exact science, a mathematical precision, which seems, alas, only too rare in the new generation of detectives!'

Japp grinned more widely.

'I don't know,' he said. 'Miller, the man who's on this case is a smart chap. You may be very sure he won't overlook a footprint, or a cigar-ash, or a crumb even. He's got eyes that see everything.'

'So, *mon ami*,' said Poirot, 'has the London sparrow. But all the same, I should not ask the little brown bird to solve the problem of Mr Davenheim.'

'Come now, monsieur, you're not going to run down the value of details as clues?'

'By no means. These things are all good in their way. The danger is they may assume undue importance. Most details are insignificant; one or two are vital. It is the brain, the little grey cells' – he tapped his forehead – 'on which one must rely. The senses mislead. One must seek the truth within – not without.'

'You don't mean to say, Monsieur Poirot, that you would undertake to solve a case without moving from your chair, do you?'

'That is exactly what I do mean – granted the facts were placed before me. I regard myself as a consulting specialist.'

Japp slapped his knee. 'Hanged if I don't take you at your word. Bet you a fiver that you can't lay your hand – or rather tell me where to lay my hand – on Mr Davenheim, dead or alive, before a week is out.' Poirot considered. '*Eh bien, mon ami*, I accept. *Le sport*, it is the passion of you English. Now – the facts.'

'On Saturday last, as is his usual custom, Mr Davenheim took the 12.40 train from Victoria to Chingside, where his palatial country seat, The Cedars, is situated. After lunch, he strolled round the grounds, and gave various directions to the gardeners. Everybody agrees that his manner was absolutely normal and as usual. After tea he put his head into his wife's boudoir, saying that he was going to stroll down to the village and post some letters. He added that he was expecting a Mr Lowen, on business. If he should come before he himself returned, he was to be shown into the study and asked to wait. Mr Davenheim then left the house by the front door, passed leisurely down the drive, and out at the gate, and – was never seen again. From that hour, he vanished completely.'

'Pretty – very pretty – altogether a charming little problem,' murmured Poirot. 'Proceed, my good friend.'

'About a quarter of an hour later a tall, dark man with a thick black moustache rang the front door-bell, and explained that he had an appointment with Mr Davenheim. He gave the name of Lowen, and in accordance with the banker's instructions was shown into the study. Nearly an hour passed. Mr Davenheim did not return. Finally Mr Lowen rang the bell, and explained that he was unable to wait any longer, as he must catch his train back to town.

'Mrs Davenheim apologized for her husband's absence, which seemed unaccountable, as she knew him to have been expecting the visitor. Mr Lowen reiterated his regrets and took his departure.

'Well, as everyone knows, Mr Davenheim did *not* return. Early on Sunday morning the police were communicated with, but could make neither head nor tail of the matter. Mr Davenheim seemed literally to have vanished into thin air. He had not been to the post office; nor had he been seen passing through the village. At the station they were positive he had not departed by any train. His own motor had not left the garage. If he had hired a car to meet him in some lonely spot, it seems almost certain that by this time, in view of the large reward offered for information, the driver of it would have come forward to tell what he knew. True, there was a small race-meeting at Entfield, five miles away, and if he had walked to that station he might have passed unnoticed in the crowd. But since then his photograph and a full description of him have been circulated in every newspaper, and nobody has been able to give any news of him. We have, of course, received many letters from all over England, but each clue, so far, has ended in disappointment.

'On Monday morning a further sensational discovery came to light. Behind a *portière* in Mr Davenheim's study stands a safe, and that safe had been broken into and rifled. The windows were fastened securely on the inside, which seems to put an ordinary burglary out of court, unless, of course, an accomplice within the house fastened them again afterwards. On the other hand, Sunday having intervened, and the household being in a state of chaos, it is likely that the burglary was committed on the Saturday, and remained undetected until Monday.'

'*Précisément*,' said Poirot dryly. 'Well, is he arrested, *ce pauvre M. Lowen*?'

Japp grinned. 'Not yet. But he's under pretty close supervision.'

Poirot nodded. 'What was taken from the safe? Have you any idea?'

'We've been going into that with the junior partner of the firm and Mrs Davenheim. Apparently there was a considerable amount in bearer bonds, and a very large sum in notes, owing to some large transaction having been just carried through. There was also a small fortune in jewellery. All Mrs Davenheim's jewels were kept in the safe. The purchasing of them had become a passion with her husband of late years, and hardly a month passed that he did not make her a present of some rare and costly gem.'

'Altogether a good haul,' said Poirot thoughtfully. 'Now, what about Lowen? Is it known what his business was with Davenheim that evening?'

'Well, the two men were apparently not on very good terms. Lowen is a speculator in quite a small way. Nevertheless, he has been able once or twice to score a coup off Davenheim in the market, though it seems they seldom or never actually met. It was a matter concerning some South American shares which led the banker to make his appointment.'

'Had Davenheim interests in South America, then?'

'I believe so. Mrs Davenheim happened to mention that he spent all last autumn in Buenos Aires.'

'Any trouble in his home life? Were the husband and wife on good terms?'

'I should say his domestic life was quite peaceful and uneventful. Mrs Davenheim is a pleasant, rather unintelligent woman. Quite a nonentity, I think.'

'Then we must not look for the solution of the mystery there. Had he any enemies?'

'He had plenty of financial rivals, and no doubt there are many people whom he has got the better of who bear him no particular goodwill. But there was no one likely to make away with him – and, if they had, where is the body?'

'Exactly. As Hastings says, bodies have a habit of coming to light with fatal persistency.'

'By the way, one of the gardeners says he saw a figure going round to the side of the house towards the rose-garden. The long trench window of the study opens on to the rose-garden, and Mr Davenheim frequently entered and left the house that way. But the man was a good way off, at work on some cucumber frames, and cannot even say whether it was the figure of his master or not. Also, he cannot fix the time with any accuracy.

116

It must have been before six, as the gardeners cease work at that time.'

'And Mr Davenheim left the house?'

'About half-past five or thereabouts.'

'What lies beyond the rose-garden?'

'A lake.'

'With a boathouse?'

'Yes, a couple of punts are kept there. I suppose you're thinking of suicide, Monsieur Poirot? Well, I don't mind telling you that Miller's going down to-morrow expressly to see that piece of water dragged. That's the kind of man he is'

Poirot smiled faintly, and turned to me. 'Hastings, I pray you, hand me that copy of *Daily Megaphone*. If I remember rightly, there is an unusually clear photograph there of the missing man.'

I rose, and found the sheet required. Poirot studied the features attentively.

'H'm!' he murmured. 'Wears his hair rather long and wavy, full moustache and pointed beard, bushy eyebrows. Eyes dark?'

'Yes.'

'Hair and beard turning grey?'

The detective nodded. 'Well, Monsieur Poirot. what have you got to say to it all? Clear as daylight, eh?'

'On the contrary, most obscure.'

The Scotland Yard man looked pleased.

'Which gives me great hopes of solving it,' finished Poirot placidly.

'Eh?'

'I find it a good sign when a case is obscure. If a thing is clear as daylight – *eh bien*, mistrust it! Someone has made it so.'

Japp shook his head almost pityingly. 'Well, each to their fancy. But it's not a bad thing to see your way clear ahead.'

'I do not see,' murmured Poirot. 'I shut my eyes – and think.'

Japp sighed. 'Well, you've got a clear week to think in.'

'And you will bring me any fresh developments that arise – the result of the labours of the hard-working and lynx-eyed Inspector Miller, for instance?'

'Certainly. That's in the bargain.'

'Seems a shame, doesn't it?' said Japp to me as I accompanied him to the door. 'Like robbing a child!' I could not help agreeing with a smile. I was still smiling as I re-entered the room.

'*Eh bien*' said Poirot immediately. 'You make fun of Papa Poirot, is it not so?' He shook his finger at me. 'You do not trust his grey cells? Ah, do not be confused! Let us discuss this little problem – incomplete as yet, I admit, but already showing one or two points of interest!'

'The lake!' I said significantly.

'And even more than the lake, the boathouse!'

I looked sidewise at Poirot. He was smiling in his most inscrutable fashion. I felt that, for the moment, it would be quite useless to question him further.

We heard nothing of Japp until the following evening, when he walked in about nine o'clock. I saw at once by his expression that he was bursting with news of some kind.

'*Eh bien,* my friend,' remarked Poirot. 'All goes well? But do not tell me that you have discovered the body of Mr Davenheim in your lake, because I shall not believe you.'

'We haven't found the body, but we did find his *clothes* – the identical clothes he was wearing that day. What do you say to that?'

'Any other clothes missing from the house?'

'No, his valet was quite positive on that point. The rest of his wardrobe is intact. There's more. We've arrested

Lowen. One of the maids, whose business it is to fasten the bedroom windows, declares that she saw Lowen coming *towards* the study through the rose-garden about a quarter-past six. That would be about ten minutes before he left the house.'

'What does he himself say to that?'

'Denied first of all that he had ever left the study. But the maid was positive, and he pretended afterwards that he had forgotten just stepping out of the window to examine an unusual species of rose. Rather a weak story! And there's fresh evidence against him come to light. Mr Davenheim always wore a thick gold ring set with a solitaire diamond on the little finger of his right hand. Well, that ring was pawned in London on Saturday night by a man called Billy Kellett! He's already known to the police – did three months last autumn for lifting an old gentleman's watch. It seems he tried to pawn the ring at no less than five different places, succeeded at the last one, got gloriously drunk on the proceeds, assaulted a policeman, and was run in in consequence. I went to Bow Street with Miller and saw him. He's sober enough now, and I don't mind admitting we pretty well frightened the life out of him, hinting he might be charged with murder. This is his yarn, and a very queer one it is.

'He was at Entfield races on Saturday, though I dare say scarfpins was his line of business, rather than betting. Anyway, he had a bad day, and was down on his luck. He was tramping along the road to Chingside, and sat down in a ditch to rest just before he got into the village. A few minutes later he noticed a man coming along the road to the village, "dark-complexioned gent, with a big moustache, one of them city toffs," is his description of the man.

'Kellett was half concealed from the road by a heap of stones. Just before he got abreast of him, the man looked quickly up and down the road, and seeing it apparently deserted he took a small object from his pocket and threw it over the hedge. Then he went on towards the station. Now, the object he had thrown over the hedge had fallen with a slight "chink" which aroused the curiosity of the human derelict in the ditch. He investigated and, after a short search, discovered the ring! That is Kellett's story. It's only fair to say that Lowen denies it utterly, and of course the word of a man like Kellett can't be relied upon in the slightest. It's within the bounds of possibility that he met Davenheim in the lane and robbed and murdered him.'

Poirot shook his head.

'Very improbable, *mon ami*. He had no means of disposing of the body. It would have been found by now. Secondly, the open way in which he pawned the ring makes it unlikely that he did murder to get it. Thirdly, your sneak-thief is rarely a murderer. Fourthly, as he has been in prison since Saturday, it would be too much of a coincidence that he is able to give so accurate a description of Lowen.'

Japp nodded. 'I don't say you're not right. But all the same, you won't get a jury to take much note of a jailbird's evidence. What seems odd to me is that Lowen couldn't find a cleverer way of disposing of the ring.'

Poirot shrugged his shoulders. 'Well, after all, if it were found in the neighbourhood, it might be argued that Davenheim himself had dropped it.'

'But why remove it from the body at all?' I cried.

'There might be a reason for that,' said Japp. 'Do you know that just beyond the lake, a little gate leads out on to the hill, and not three minutes' walk brings you to – what do you think? – a *lime kiln*.'

'Good heavens' I cried. 'You mean that the lime which destroyed the body would be powerless to affect the metal of the ring?'

'Exactly.'

'It seems to me,' I said, 'that that explains everything. What a horrible crime!'

By common consent we both turned and looked at Poirot. He seemed lost in reflection, his brow knitted, as though with some supreme mental effort. I felt at last his keen intellect was asserting itself. What would his first words be? We were not long left in doubt. With a sigh, the tension of his attitude relaxed and turning to Japp, he asked:

'Have you any idea, my friend, whether Mr and Mrs Davenheim occupied the same bedroom?'

The question seemed so ludicrously inappropriate that for a moment we both stared in silence. Then Japp burst into a laugh. 'Good Lord, Monsieur Poirot, I thought you were coming out with something startling. As to your question, I'm sure I don't know.'

'You could find out?' asked Poirot with curious persistence.

'Oh, certainly – if you *really* want to know.'

'*Merci, mon ami.* I should be obliged if you would make a point of it.'

Japp stared at him a few minutes longer, but Poirot seemed to have forgotten us both. The detective shook his head sadly at me, and murmuring, 'Poor old fellow! War's been too much for him!' gently withdrew from the room.

As Poirot seemed sunk in a daydream, I took a sheet of paper, and amused myself by scribbling notes upon it. My friend's voice aroused me. He had come out of his reverie, and was looking brisk and alert.

'*Que faites-vous là, mon ami?*'

'I was jotting down what occurred to me as the main points of interest in this affair.'

'You become methodical – at last!' said Poirot approvingly.

I concealed my pleasure. 'Shall I read them to you?'

'By all means.'

I cleared my throat.

' "One: All the evidence points to Lowen having been the man who forced the safe.

' "Two: He had a grudge against Davenheim.

' "Three: He lied in his first statement that he had never left the study.

' "Four: If you accept Billy Kellett's story as true, Lowen is unmistakably implicated." '

I paused. 'Well?' I asked, for I felt that I had put my finger on all the vital facts.

Poirot looked at me pityingly, shaking his head very gently. '*Mon pauvre ami*! But it is that you have not the gift The important detail, you appreciate him never! Also, your reasoning is false.'

'How?'

'Let me take your four points.'

'One: Mr Lowen could not possibly know that he would have the chance to open the safe. He came for a business interview. He could not know beforehand that Mr Davenheim would be absent posting a letter, and that he would consequently be alone in the study!'

'He might have seized the opportunity,' I suggested.

'And the tools? City gentlemen do not carry round housebreaker's tools on the off chance! And one could not cut into that safe with penknife, *bien entendu*!'

'Well, what about Number Two?'

'You say Lowen had a grudge against Mr Davenheim. What you mean is that he had once or twice got the better of him. And presumably those transactions were entered into with the view of benefiting himself. In any case you do not as a rule bear a grudge against a man you have got the better of – it is more likely to be the other way about. Whatever grudge there might have been would have been on Mr Davenheim's side.'

'Well, you can't deny that he lied about never having left the study?'

'No. But he may have been frightened. Remember, the missing man's clothes had just been discovered in the lake. Of course, as usual, he would have done better to speak the truth.'

'And the fourth point?'

'I grant you that. If Kellett's story is true, Lowen is undeniably implicated. That is what makes the affair so very interesting.'

'Then I *did* appreciate one vital fact?'

'Perhaps – but you have entirely overlooked the two most important points, the ones which undoubtedly hold the clue to the whole matter.'

'And pray, what are they?'

'One, the passion which has grown upon Mr Davenheim in the last few years for buying jewellery. Two, his trip to Buenos Aires last autumn.'

'Poirot, you are joking?'

'I am serious. Ah, sacred thunder, but I hope Japp will not forget my little commission.'

But the detective, entering into the spirit of the joke, had remembered it so well that a telegram was handed to Poirot about eleven o'clock the next day. At his request I opened it and read it out:

' "Husband and wife have occupied separate rooms since last winter." '

'Aha!' cried Poirot. 'And now we are in mid June! All is solved!'

I stared at him.

'You have no moneys in the bank of Davenheim and Salmon, *mon ami*?'

'No,' I said wondering. 'Why?'

'Because I should advise you to withdraw it – before it is too late.'

'Why, what do you expect?'

'I expect a big smash in a few days – perhaps sooner. Which reminds me, we will return the compliment of a *dèpêche* to Japp. A pencil, I pray you, and a form. *Voilá!* "Advise you to withdraw any money deposited with firm in question." That will intrigue him, the good Japp! His eyes will open wide – wide! He will not comprehend in the slightest – until tomorrow, or the next day!'

I remained sceptical, but the morrow forced me to render tribute to my friend's remarkable powers. In every paper was a huge headline telling of the sensational failure of the Davenheim bank. The disappearance of the famous financier took on a totally different aspect in the light of the revelation of the financial affairs of the bank.

Before we were half-way through breakfast, the door flew open and Japp rushed in. In his left hand was a paper; in his right was Poirot's telegram, which he banged down on the table in front of my friend.

'How did you know, Monsieur Poirot? How the blazes could you know?'

Poirot smiled placidly at him. 'Ah, *mon ami*, after your wire, it was a certainty! From the commencement, see you, it struck me that the safe burglary was somewhat remarkable. Jewels, ready money, bearer bonds – all so conveniently arranged for – whom? Well, the good Monsieur Davenheim was of those who "look after Number One" as your saying goes! It seemed almost certain that it was arranged for – himself! Then his passion of late years for buying jewellery! How simple! The funds he embezzled, he converted into jewels, very likely replacing them in turn with paste duplicates, and so he put away in a safe place, under another name, a considerable fortune to be enjoyed all in good time when everyone has been thrown off the track. His arrangements completed, he makes an appointment with Mr Lowen (who has been imprudent enough in the past to cross the great man once or twice), drills a hole in the safe, leaves orders that the guest is to be shown into the study, and walks out of the house – where?' Poirot stopped, and stretched out his hand for another boiled egg. He frowned. 'It is really insupportable,' he murmured, 'that every hen lays an egg of a different size What symmetry can there be on the breakfast table? At least they should sort them in dozens at the shop!'

'Never mind the eggs,' said Japp impatiently. 'Let 'em lay 'em square if they like. Tell us where our customer went to when he left The Cedars – that is, if you know!'

'*Eh bien,* he went to his hiding place. Ah, this Monsieur Davenheim, there may be some malformation in his grey cells, but they are of the first quality!'

'Do you know where he is hiding?'

'Certainly! It is most ingenious.'

'For the Lord's sake, tell us, then!'

Poirot gently collected every fragment of shell from his plate, placed them in the egg-cup, and reversed the empty egg-shell on top of them. This little operation concluded, he smiled on the neat effect, and then beamed affectionately on us both.

'Come, my friends, you are men of intelligence. Ask yourself the question I asked myself. "If I were this man, where should *I* hide?" Hastings, what do you say?'

'Well,' I said, 'I'm rather inclined to think I'd not do a bolt at all. I'd stay in London – in the heart of things, travel by tubes and buses; ten to one I'd never be recognized. There's safety in a crowd.'

Poirot turned inquiringly to Japp.

'I don't agree. Get clear away at once – that's the only chance. I would have had plenty of time to prepare things beforehand. I'd have a yacht waiting, with steam up, and I'd be off to one of the most out-of-the-way corners of the world before the hue and cry began!'

We both looked at Poirot. 'What do *you* say, monsieur?'

For a moment he remained silent. Then a very curious smile flitted across his face.

'My friends, if *I* were hiding from the police, do you know *where* I should hide? *In a prison!*'

'*What?*'

'You are seeking Monsieur Davenheim in order to put him in prison, so you never dream of looking to see if he may not be already there!'

'What do you mean?'

'You tell me Madame Davenheim is not a very intelligent woman. Nevertheless I think if you took her up to Bow Street and confronted her with the man Billy Kellett she would recognize him! In spite of the fact that he has shaved his beard and moustache and those bushy eyebrows, and has cropped his hair close. A woman nearly always knows her husband, though the rest of the world may be deceived.'

'Billy Kellett? But he's known to the police!'

'Did I not tell you Davenheim was a clever man? He prepared his alibi long beforehand. He was not in Buenos Aires last autumn – he was creating the character of Billy Kellett, "doing three months", so that the police should have no suspicions when the time came. He was playing, remember, for a large fortune, as well as liberty. It was worth while doing the thing thoroughly. Only – '

'Yes?'

'*Eh bien*, afterwards he had to wear a false beard and wig, had to *make up as himself again*, and to sleep with a false beard is not easy – it invites detection! He cannot risk continuing to share the chamber of madame his wife. You found out for me that for the last six months, or ever since his supposed return from Buenos Aires, he and Mrs Davenheim occupied separate rooms. Then I was sure! Everything fitted in. The gardener who fancied he saw his master going round to the side of the house was quite right. He went to the boathouse, donned his "tramp" clothes, which you may be sure had been safely hidden from the eyes of his valet, dropped the others in the lake, and proceeded to carry out his plan by pawning the ring in an obvious manner, and then assaulting a policeman, getting himself safely into the haven of Bow Street, where nobody would ever dream of looking for him!'

'It's impossible,' murmured Japp.

'Ask Madame,' said my friend, smiling.

The next day a registered letter lay beside Poirot's plate. He opened it and a five-pound note fluttered out. My friend's brow puckered.

'*Ah, sacré*! But what shall I do with it? I have much remorse! *Ce pauvre Japp*? Ah, an idea! We will have a little dinner, we three! That consoles me. It was really too easy. I am ashamed. I, who would not rob a child – *mille tonnerres*! *Mon ami*, what have you, that you laugh so heartily?'

THE ADVENTURE OF THE CHEAP FLAT

So far, in the cases which I have recorded, Poirot's investigations have started from the central fact, whether murder or robbery, and have proceeded from thence by a process of logical deduction to the final triumphant unravelling. In the events I am now about to chronicle a remarkable chain of circumstances led from the apparently trivial incidents which first attracted Poirot's attention to the sinister happenings which completed a most unusual case.

I had been spending the evening with an old friend of mine, Gerald Parker. There had been, perhaps, about half a dozen people there besides my host and myself, and the talk fell, as it was bound to do sooner or later wherever Parker found himself, on the subject of house-hunting in London. Houses and flats were Parker's special hobby. Since the end of the War, he had occupied at least half a dozen different flats and maisonettes. No sooner was he settled anywhere than he would light unexpectedly upon a new find, and would forthwith depart bag and baggage. His moves were nearly always accomplished at a slight pecuniary gain, for he had a shrewd business head, but it was sheer love of the sport that actuated him, and not a desire to make money at it. We listened to Parker for some time with the respect of the novice for the expert. Then it was our turn, and a perfect babel of tongues was let loose. Finally the floor was left to Mrs Robinson, a charming little bride who was there with her husband. I had never met them before, as Robinson was only a recent acquaintance of Parker's.

'Talking of flats,' she said, 'have you heard of our piece of luck, Mr Parker? We've got a flat – at last! In Montagu Mansions.'

'Well,' said Parker, 'I've always said there are plenty of flats – at a price!'

'Yes, but this isn't at a price. It's dirt cheap. Eighty pounds a year!'

'But – but Montagu Mansions is just off Knightsbridge, isn't it? Big handsome building. Or are you talking of a poor relation of the same name stuck in the slums somewhere?'

'No, it's the Knightsbridge one. That's what makes it so wonderful.'

'Wonderful is the word! It's a blinking miracle. But there must be a catch somewhere. Big premium, I suppose?'

'No premium!'

'No prem – oh, hold my head, somebody!' groaned Parker.

'But we've got to buy the furniture,' continued Mrs Robinson.

'Ah' Parker bristled up. 'I knew there was a catch!'

'For fifty pounds. And it's beautifully furnished!'

'I give it up,' said Parker. 'The present occupants must be lunatics with a taste for philanthropy.'

Mrs Robinson was looking a little troubled. A little pucker appeared between her dainty brows.

'It *is* queer, isn't it? You don't think that – that – the place is *haunted*?'

'Never heard of a haunted flat,' declared Parker decisively.

'No-o.' Mrs Robinson appeared far from convinced. 'But there were several things about it all that struck me as – well, queer.'

'For instance – ' I suggested.

'Ah,' said Parker, 'our criminal expert's attention is aroused! Unburden yourself to him, Mrs Robinson. Hastings is a great unraveller of mysteries.'

I laughed, embarrassed, but not wholly displeased with the rôle thrust upon me.

'Oh, not really queer, Captain Hastings, but when we went to the agents, Stosser and Paul – we hadn't tried them before because they only have the expensive Mayfair flats, but we thought at any rate it would do no harm – everything they offered us was four and five hundred a year, or else huge premiums, and then, just as we were going, they mentioned that they had a flat at eighty, but that they doubted if it would be any good our going there, because it had been on their books some time and they had sent so many people to see it that it was almost sure to be taken – "snapped up" as the clerk put it – only people were so tiresome in not letting them know, and then they went on sending, and people get annoyed at being sent to a place that had, perhaps, been let some time.'

Mrs Robinson paused for some much needed breath, and then continued:

'We thanked him, and said that we quite understood it would probably be no good, but that we should like an order all the same – just in case. And we went there straight away in a taxi, for, after all, you never know. No 4 was on the second floor, and just as we were waiting for the lift, Elsie Ferguson – she's a friend of mine, Captain Hastings, and they are looking for a flat too – came hurrying down the stairs. "Ahead of you for once, my dear," she said. "But it's no good. It's already let." That seemed to finish it, but – well, as John said, the place was very cheap, we could afford to give more, and perhaps if we offered a premium. A horrid thing to do, of course, and I feel quite ashamed of telling you, but you know what flat-hunting is.'

I assured her that I was well aware that in the struggle for house-room the baser side of human nature frequently triumphed over the higher, and that the well-known rule of dog eat dog always applied.

'So we went up and, would you believe it, the flat wasn't let at all. We were shown over it by the maid, and then we saw the mistress, and the thing was settled then and there. Immediate possession and fifty pounds for the furniture. We signed the agreement next day, and we are to move in tomorrow!' Mrs Robinson paused triumphantly.

'And what about Mrs Ferguson?' asked Parker. 'Let's have your deductions, Hastings.'

' "Obvious, my dear Watson," ' I quoted lightly. 'She went to the wrong flat.'

'Oh, Captain Hastings, how clever of you!' cried Mrs Robinson admiringly.

I rather wished Poirot had been there. Sometimes I have the feeling that he rather underestimates my capabilities.

The whole thing was rather amusing, and I propounded the thing as a mock problem to Poirot on the following morning. He seemed interested, and questioned me rather narrowly as to the rents of flats in various localities.

'A curious story,' he said thoughtfully. 'Excuse me, Hastings, I must take a short stroll.'

When he returned, about an hour later, his eyes were gleaming with a peculiar excitement. He laid his stick on the table, and brushed the nap of his hat with his usual tender care before he spoke.

'It is as well, *mon ami*, that we have no affairs of

131

moment on hand. We can devote ourselves wholly to the present investigation.'

'What investigation are you talking about?'

'The remarkable cheapness of your friend, Mrs Robinson's, new flat.'

'Poirot, you are not serious!'

'I am most serious. Figure to yourself, my friend, that the real rent of those flats is £350. I have just ascertained that from the landlord's agents. And yet this particular flat is being sublet at eighty pounds! Why?'

'There must be something wrong with it. Perhaps it is haunted, as Mrs Robinson suggested.'

Poirot shook his head in a dissatisfied manner.

'Then again how curious it is that her friend tells her the flat is let, and, when she goes up, behold, it is not so at all!'

'But surely you agree with me that the other woman must have gone to the wrong flat. That is the only possible solution.'

'You may or may not be right on that point, Hastings. The fact still remains that numerous other applicants were sent to see it, and yet, in spite of its remarkable cheapness, it was still in the market when Mrs Robinson arrived.'

'That shows that there *must* be something wrong about it.'

'Mrs Robinson did not seem to notice anything amiss. Very curious, is it not? Did she impress you as being a truthful woman, Hastings?'

'She was a delightful creature!'

'*Evidemment*! since she renders you incapable of replying to my question. Describe her to me, then.'

'Well, she's tall and fair; her hair's really a beautiful shade of auburn – '

'Always you have had a penchant for auburn hair!' murmured Poirot. 'But continue.'

'Blue eyes and a very nice complexion and – well, that's all, I think,' I concluded lamely.

'And her husband?'

'Oh, he's quite a nice fellow – nothing startling.'

'Dark or fair?'

'I don't know – betwixt and between, and just an ordinary sort of face.'

Poirot nodded.

'Yes, there are hundreds of these average men – and anyway, you bring more sympathy and appreciation to your description of women. Do you know anything about these people? Does Parker know them well?'

'They are just recent acquaintances, I believe. But surely, Poirot, you don't think for an instant – '

Poirot raised his hand.

'*Tout doucement, mon ami.* Have I said that I think anything? All I say is – it is a curious story. And there is nothing to throw light upon it; except perhaps the lady's name, eh, Hastings?'

'Her name is Stella,' I said stiffly, 'but I don't see – '

Poirot interrupted me with a tremendous chuckle. Something seemed to be amusing him vastly.

'And Stella means a star, does it not? Famous!'

'What on earth – ?'

'And stars give light! *Voilà*! Calm yourself, Hastings. Do not put on that air of injured dignity. Come, we will go to Montagu Mansions and make a few inquiries.'

I accompanied him, nothing loath. The Mansions were a handsome block of buildings in excellent repair. A uniformed porter was sunning himself on the threshold, and it was to him that Poirot addressed himself:

'Pardon, but could you tell me if a Mr and Mrs Robinson reside here?'

The porter was a man of few words and apparently of a sour or suspicious disposition. He hardly looked at us and grunted out:

'No. 4. Second floor.'

'I thank you. Can you tell me how long they have been here?'

'Six months.'

I started forward in amazement, conscious as I did so of Poirot's malicious grin.

'Impossible,' I cried. 'You must be making a mistake.'

'Six months.'

'Are you sure? The lady I mean is tall and fair with reddish gold hair and – '

'That's 'er,' said the porter. 'Come in the Michaelmas quarter, they did. Just six months ago.'

He appeared to lose interest in us and retreated slowly up the hall. I followed Poirot outside.

'*Eh bien*, Hastings?' my friend demanded slyly. 'Are you so sure now that delightful women always speak the truth?'

I did not reply.

Poirot had steered his way into Brompton Road before I asked him what he was going to do and where we were going.

'To the house agents, Hastings. I have a great desire to have a flat in Montagu Mansions. If I am not mistaken, several interesting things will take place there before long.'

We were fortunate in our quest. No. 8, on the fourth floor, was to be let furnished at ten guineas a week, Poirot promptly took it for a month. Outside in the street again, he silenced my protests:

'But I make money nowadays Why should I not indulge a whim? By the way, Hastings, have you a revolver?'

'Yes – somewhere,' I answered, slightly thrilled. 'Do you think – '

'That you will need it? It is quite possible. The idea

pleases you, I see. Always the spectacular and romantic appeals to you.'

The following day saw us installed in our temporary home. The flat was pleasantly furnished. It occupied the same position in the building as that of the Robinsons, but was two floors higher.

The day after our installation was a Sunday. In the afternoon, Poirot left the front door ajar, and summoned me hastily as a bang reverberated from somewhere below.

'Look over the banisters. Are those your friends? Do not let them see you.'

I craned my neck over the staircase.

'That's them,' I declared in an ungrammatical whisper.

'Good. Wait awhile.'

About half an hour later, a young woman emerged in brilliant and varied clothing. With a sigh of satisfaction, Poirot tiptoed back into the flat.

'*C'est ça*. After the master and mistress, the maid. The flat should now be empty.'

'What are we going to do?' I asked uneasily.

Poirot had trotted briskly into the scullery and was hauling at the rope of the coal-lift.

'We are about to descend after the method of the dustbins,' he explained cheerfully. 'No one will observe us. The Sunday concert, the Sunday "afternoon out", and finally the Sunday nap after the Sunday dinner of England – *le rosbif* – all these will distract attention from the doings of Hercule Poirot. Come, my friend.'

He stepped into the rough wooden contrivance and I followed him gingerly.

'Are we going to break into the flat?' I asked dubiously.

Poirot's answer was not too reassuring:

'Not precisely today,' he replied.

Pulling on the rope, we descended slowly till we reached the second floor. Poirot uttered an exclamation of satisfaction as he perceived that the wooden door into the scullery was open.

'You observe? Never do they bolt these doors in the daytime. And yet anyone could mount or descend as we have done. At night, yes – though not always then – and it is against that that we are going to make provision.'

He had drawn some tools from his pocket as he spoke, and at once set deftly to work, his object being to arrange the bolt so that it could be pulled back from the lift. The operation only occupied about three minutes. Then Poirot returned the tools to his pocket, and we re-ascended once more to our own domain.

On Monday Poirot was out all day, but when he returned in the evening he flung himself into his chair with a sigh of satisfaction.

'Hastings, shall I recount to you a little history? A story after your own heart and which will remind you of your favourite cinema?'

'Go ahead,' I laughed. 'I presume that it is a true story, not one of your efforts of fancy.'

'It is true enough. Inspector Japp of Scotland Yard will vouch for its accuracy, since it was through his kind offices that it came to my ears. Listen, Hastings. A little over six months ago some important Naval plans were stolen from an American Government department. They showed the position of some of the most important Harbour defences, and would be worth a considerable sum to any foreign Government – that of Japan, for example. Suspicion fell upon a young man named Luigi Valdarno, an Italian by birth, who was employed in a minor capacity in the Department and who was missing at the same time as the papers. Whether Luigi Valdarno was the thief or not, he was found two days later on the East

Side in New York, shot dead. The papers were not on him. Now for some time past Luigi Valdarno had been going about with a Miss Elsa Hardt, a young concert singer who had recently appeared and who lived with a brother in an apartment in Washington. Nothing was known of the antecedents of Miss Elsa Hardt, and she disappeared suddenly about the time of Valdarno's death. There are reasons for believing that she was in reality an accomplished international spy who has done much nefarious work under various aliases. The American Secret Service, while doing their best to trace her, also kept an eye upon certain insignificant Japanese gentlemen living in Washington. They felt pretty certain that, when Elsa Hardt had covered her tracks sufficiently, she would approach the gentlemen in question. One of them left suddenly for England a fortnight ago. On the face of it, therefore, it would seem that Elsa Hardt is in England.' Poirot paused, and then added softly: 'The official description of Elsa Hardt is: Height 5 ft 7, eyes blue, hair auburn, fair complexion, nose straight, no special distinguishing marks.'

'Mrs Robinson!' I gasped.

'Well, there is a chance of it, anyhow,' amended Poirot. 'Also I learn that a swarthy man, a foreigner of some kind, was inquiring about the occupants of No. 4 only this morning. Therefore, *mon ami*, I fear that you must forswear your beauty sleep tonight, and join me in my all-night vigil in that flat below – armed with that excellent revolver of yours, *bien entendu*!'

'Rather,' I cried with enthusiasm. 'When shall we start?'

'The hour of midnight is both solemn and suitable, I fancy. Nothing is likely to occur before then.'

At twelve o'clock precisely, we crept cautiously into the coal-lift and lowered ourselves to the second floor. Under Poirot's manipulation, the wooden door quickly swung inwards, and we climbed into the flat. From the scullery we passed into the kitchen where we established ourselves comfortably in two chairs with the door into the hall ajar.

'Now we have but to wait,' said Poirot contentedly, closing his eyes.

To me, the waiting appeared endless. I was terrified of going to sleep. Just when it seemed to me that I had been there about eight hours – and had, as I found out afterwards, in reality been exactly one hour and twenty minutes – a faint scratching sound came to my ears. Poirot's hand touched mine. I rose, and together we moved carefully in the direction of the hall. The noise came from there. Poirot placed his lips to my ear.

'Outside the front door. They are cutting out the lock. When I give the word, not before, fall upon him from behind and hold him fast. Be careful, he will have a knife.'

Presently there was a rending sound, and a little circle of light appeared through the door. It was extinguished immediately and then the door was slowly opened. Poirot and I flattened ourselves against the wall. I heard a man's breathing as he passed us. Then he flashed on his torch, and as he did so, Poirot hissed in my ear:

'*Allez.*'

We sprang together, Poirot with a quick movement enveloped the intruder's head with a light woollen scarf whilst I pinioned his arms. The whole affair was quick and noiseless. I twisted a dagger from his hand, and as Poirot brought down the scarf from his eyes, whilst keeping it wound tightly round his mouth, I jerked up my revolver where he could see it and understand that resistance was useless. As he ceased to struggle Poirot put his mouth close to his ear and began to whisper rapidly. After a minute the man nodded. Then enjoining silence with a movement of the hand, Poirot led the way out of the flat and down the stairs. Our captive followed, and I brought up the rear with the revolver. When we were out in the street, Poirot turned to me.

'There is a taxi waiting just round the corner. Give me the revolver. We shall not need it now.'

'But if this fellow tries to escape?'

Poirot smiled.

'He will not.'

I returned in a minute with the waiting taxi. The scarf had been unwound from the stranger's face, and I gave a start of surprise.

'He's not a Jap,' I ejaculated in a whisper to Poirot.

'Observation was always your strong point, Hastings Nothing escapes you. No, the man is not a Jap. He is an Italian.'

We got into the taxi, and Poirot gave the driver an address in St John's Wood. I was by now completely fogged. I did not like to ask Poirot where we were going in front of our captive, and strove in vain to obtain some light upon the proceedings.

We alighted at the door of a small house standing back from the road. A returning wayfarer, slightly drunk, was lurching along the pavement and almost collided with Poirot, who said something sharply to him which I did not catch. All three of us went up the steps of the house. Poirot rang the bell and motioned us to stand a little aside. There was no answer and he rang again and then seized the knocker which he plied for some minutes vigorously.

A light appeared suddenly above the fanlight, and the door opened cautiously a little way.

'What the devil do you want?' a man's voice demanded harshly.

'I want the doctor. My wife is taken ill.'

'There's no doctor here.'

The man prepared to shut the door, but Poirot thrust

his foot in adroitly. He became suddenly a perfect carica-
ture of an infuriated Frenchman.

'What you say, there is no doctor? I will have the law
of you. You must come! I will stay here and ring and
knock all night.'

'My dear sir – ' The door was opened again, the man,
clad in a dressing-gown and slippers, stepped forward to
pacify Poirot with an uneasy glance round.

'I will call the police.'

Poirot prepared to descend the steps.

'No, don't do that for Heaven's sake!' The man dashed
after him.

With a neat push Poirot sent him staggering down the
steps. In another minute all three of us were inside the
door and it was pushed to and bolted.

'Quick – in here.' Poirot led the way into the nearest
room, switching on the light as he did so. 'And you –
behind the curtain.'

'Si, Signor,' said the Italian and slid rapidly behind
the full folds of rose-coloured velvet which draped the
embrasure of the window.

Not a minute too soon. Just as he disappeared from
view a woman rushed into the room. She was tall with
reddish hair and held a scarlet kimono round her slender
form.

'Where is my husband?' she cried, with a quick frightened glance. 'Who are you?'

Poirot stepped forward with a bow.

'It is to be hoped your husband will not suffer from
a chill. I observed that he had slippers on his feet, and
that his dressing-gown was a warm one.'

'Who are you? What are you doing in my house?'

'It is true that none of us have the pleasure of your
acquaintance, madame. It is especially to be regretted as
one of our number has come specially from New York
in order to meet you.'

The curtains parted and the Italian stepped out. To my horror I observed that he was brandishing my revolver, which Poirot must doubtless have put down through inadvertence in the cab.

The woman gave a piercing scream and turned to fly, but Poirot was standing in front of the closed door.

'Let me by,' she shrieked. 'He will murder me.'

'Who was it dat croaked Luigi Valdarno?' asked the Italian hoarsely, brandishing the weapon, and sweeping each one of us with it. We dared not move.

'My God, Poirot, this is awful. What shall we do?' I cried.

'You will oblige me by refraining from talking so much, Hastings. I can assure you that our friend will not shoot until I give the word.'

'Youse sure o' dat, eh?' said the Italian, leering unpleasantly.

It was more than I was, but the woman turned to Poirot like a flash.

'What is it you want?'

Poirot bowed.

'I do not think it is necessary to insult Miss Elsa Hardt's intelligence by telling her.'

With a swift movement, the woman snatched up a big black velvet cat which served as a cover for the telephone.

'They are stitched in the lining of that.'

'Clever,' murmured Poirot appreciatively. He stood aside from the door. 'Good evening, madame. I will detain your friend from New York whilst you make your getaway.'

'Whatta fool!' roared the big Italian, and raising the revolver he fired point-blank at the woman's retreating figure just as I flung myself upon him.

But the weapon merely clicked harmlessly and Poirot's voice rose in mild reproof.

'Never will you trust your old friend, Hastings. I do not care for my friends to carry loaded pistols about with them and never would I permit a mere acquaintance to do so. No, no, *mon ami*.' This to the Italian who was swearing hoarsely. Poirot continued to address him in a tone of mild reproof: 'See now, what I have done for you. I have saved you from being hanged. And do not think that our beautiful lady will escape. No, no, the house is watched, back and front. Straight into the arms of the police they will go. Is not that a beautiful and consoling thought? Yes, you may leave the room now. But be careful – be very careful. I – Ah, he is gone! And my friend Hastings looks at me with eyes of reproach. But it's all so simple! It was clear, from the first, that out of several hundred, probably, applicants for No. 4 Montagu Mansions, only the Robinsons were considered suitable. Why? What was there that singled them out from the rest – at practically a glance. Their appearance? Possibly, but it was not so unusual. Their name, then!'

'But there's nothing unusual about the name of Robinson,' I cried. 'It's quite a common name.'

'Ah! *Sapristi*, but exactly! That was the point. Elsa Hardt and her husband, or brother or whatever he really is, come from New York, and take a flat in the name of Mr and Mrs Robinson. Suddenly they learn that one of these secret societies, the Mafia, or the Camorra, to which doubtless Luigi Valdarno belonged, is on their track. What do they do? They hit on a scheme of transparent simplicity. Evidently they knew that their pursuers were not personally acquainted with either of them. What, then, can be simpler? They offer the flat at an absurdly low rental. Of the thousands of young couples in London looking for flats, there cannot fail to be several Robinsons. It is only a matter of waiting. If you will look at the name of Robinson in the telephone directory, you will realize that a fair-haired Mrs Robinson was pretty sure to come along sooner or later. Then what will happen? The avenger arrives. He knows the name, he knows the address. He strikes! All is over, vengeance is satisfied, and Miss Elsa Hardt has escaped by the skin of her teeth once more. By the way, Hastings, you must present me to the real Mrs Robinson – that delightful and truthful creature! What will they think when they find their flat has been broken into! We must hurry back. Ah, that sounds like Japp and his friends arriving.'

A mighty tattoo sounded on the knocker.

'How do you know this address?' I asked as I followed Poirot out into the hall. 'Oh, of course, you had the first Mrs Robinson followed when she left the other flat.'

'*A la bonne heure*, Hastings. You use your grey cells at last. Now for a little surprise for Japp.'

Softly unbolting the door, he stuck the cat's head round the edge and ejaculated a piercing 'Miaow'.

The Scotland Yard inspector, who was standing outside with another man, jumped in spite of himself.

'Oh, it's only Monsieur Poirot at one of his little jokes!' he exclaimed, as Poirot's head followed that of the cat. 'Let us in, moosior.'

'You have our friends safe and sound?'

'Yes, we've got the birds all right, But they hadn't got the goods with them.'

'I see. So you come to search. Well, I am about to depart with Hastings, but I should like to give you a little lecture upon the history and habits of the domestic cat.'

'For the Lord's sake, have you gone completely balmy?'

'The cat,' declaimed Poirot, 'was worshipped by the ancient Egyptians. It is still regarded as a symbol of good luck if a black cat crosses your path. This cat crossed your path to-night, Japp. To speak of the interior of any animal or any person is not, I know, considered polite in England. But the interior of this cat is perfectly delicate. I refer to the lining.'

With a sudden grunt, the second man seized the cat from Poirot's hand.

'Oh, I forgot to introduce you,' said Japp. 'Mr Poirot, this is Mr Burt of the United States Secret Service.'

The American's trained fingers had felt what he was looking for. He held out his hand, and for a moment speech failed him. Then he rose to the occasion.

'Pleased to meet you,' said Mr Burt.